Triangulation: Dark Glass

The 2009 Edition of PARSEC Ink's Annual
Confluence of Speculative Fiction

ISBN: 978-0-578-03103-3

Cover Art: Vincent Chong

Assistant Fiction Editors: Joseph Benedetto, Jamie Lackey, Bill Moran, Deanna Hardin

Senior Fiction Editor: Pete Butler

PARSEC Ink is a subsidiary of the literary organization PARSEC. For more information, visit our website at ParsecInk.org.

PARSEC Ink
PO Box 3681
Pittsburgh, PA 15230-3681

Contents

The Milton Feinhoff Problem

Mark Onspaugh

One bright spring morning, Milton Feinhoff came downstairs to find himself eating an enormous stack of waffles. Not only was it disconcerting to find some doppelganger at his table, it was nauseating to see him wolfing down waffles; Milton had always hated waffles.

Waffle Milton was also surprised by the appearance of himself, and put down his fork.

They regarded one another.

Aside from dress, Waffle Milton in work clothes and Non-Waffle Milton in tee shirt and jeans, they appeared identical.

Both looked around, but there was no evidence of a mirror or projection screen. A hologram of this sophistication seemed unlikely, though the military might have one. Milton Feinhoff (both) thought it unlikely they would waste such technology on him.

They studied each other carefully, looking for mask seams or makeup smudges.

"Robot," they said simultaneously, then shook their heads, each pulling up his shirt to reveal the pale Milton Feinhoff paunch with a mole inside the navel and a cluster of hairs above and below.

"Android!" they both shouted quickly. It was a silly notion, there were certainly no Milton Feinhoff androids being fabricated somewhere. If they even existed, such things would surely be reserved for world leaders and attractive celebrities.

In the kitchen, Waffle Milton poured them fresh coffee while Non-Waffle Milton got himself a bowl of muesli.

"What high school did you attend," they demanded simultaneously.

"James Monroe High, go Vikings!" both shouted.

Both pulled quarters from their pockets, both flipped them, both called "heads."

Both fumbled the catch and both quarters rolled under the stove.

For the next two hours they grilled each other relentlessly on childhood, girlfriends, favorite movies, and embarrassing moments involving sex and/or acne.

They were identical in every non-clothing, non-waffle way.

Waffle Milton pointed to his double's casual dress. "Why weren't you going to the office today?"

Now they were on to something!

"I felt like I had the flu."

"Me too, but I decided to go in."

"So," Waffle Milton began, "whatever separates us. . . ."

"Began with that decision," Non-Waffle Milton finished.

"Unless one of us is from the future," Waffle Milton said.

Neither could remember any future events. So much for the stock tips of tomorrow.

"Quantum mechanics," they said in chorus, and each nodded sagely.

The truth was, neither of them knew much about quantum theory or advanced physics or the goopy meta-nougat underneath reality, save what they had seen on the Discovery Channel, and Milton Feinhoff (both) had often fallen asleep during such programs, waking up bombarded by ads for *Girls Gone Wild.*

Still, they worked it out the best they could, deciding that some cosmic rupture had allowed one of them to spill into the wrong Earth.

"One of us doesn't belong here," they both said at once.

"And what about Janice?" they asked.

Milton Feinhoff and Janice Higashida-Feinhoff had a good marriage. If the duplication was permanent, how would they reconcile one Janice?

"I wonder if there is a world somewhere that has a Janice and is missing a Milton Feinhoff," Waffle Milton asked. He wasn't about to admit it to Non-Waffle Milton, but he was beginning to suspect that he was the one who didn't belong. The coffee seemed to have an odd taste to it, and the house felt kind of cold . . . alien to him.

For his part, Non-Waffle Milton was also wondering whether or not he belonged on this particular Earth. A place where he liked waffles? Ridiculous! And he wasn't that crazy about the wallpaper, either.

Both Milton Feinhoffs smiled at the other uneasily, wondering what other perils this world might have to offer.

The door opened, and Janice entered.

The minute they saw her, all doubts melted away. Here was Janice, her black hair lustrous in the morning light, her brown eyes large and mischievous.

Here was Janice. He *was* home.

The other Milton Feinhoff must be the intruder.

Janice looked up, saw Waffle Milton and Non-Waffle Milton, and shrieked.

Then Milton Feinhoff entered the house behind Janice, wearing a plaid sportscoat that neither Waffle nor Non-Waffle Milton liked.

The three Miltons regarded each other silently as Janice looked on in horror.

A fourth Milton shambled downstairs, dressed only in boxer shorts and a robe. He was blowing his nose and coughing, and looked terrible.

Janice bolted upstairs, dodging a Milton Feinhoff in jogging clothes. His arrival coincided with a Milton Feinhoff who came in from the backyard covered in mud and peat moss.

Janice locked herself in the upstairs bathroom, sure she was having a psychotic break.

Flu Milton, thinking he was suffering the effects of his medication, went back to bed, ignoring the protests of his fellow Miltons.

The house began to fill up with Milton Feinhoffs.

There were Milton Feinhoffs in wetsuits, and others dressed for the opera. There were some in clown suits and others in unwashed rags. One sported a rakish fedora, another a fez, still another a turban.

As their numbers multiplied, differences beyond clothing began to manifest themselves.

Some Miltons were slightly taller, or shorter. Some slightly thinner or heavier. One had a shaved head, another a beard. One wore glasses and another had an eye patch.

Soon the population of Milton Feinhoffs in the house numbered one hundred, and they were all ravenous. They pooled their money for beer and thirty-one pizzas.

Thirty pepperoni and mushroom, one with pineapple and Canadian bacon.

The two who had opted for pineapple and Canadian bacon were silently singled out by the other ninety-eight as candidates for dimensional expulsion, if such a thing were possible.

Waffle Milton, Non-Waffle Milton, and Sportscoat Milton spent a good hour convincing Janice she was not crazy. Sportscoat Milton suggested she might be able to tell who was the "real deal" by kissing them, but this just made Janice cry.

Waffle and Non-Waffle Milton held a private confab in the laundry room. They agreed that some means would have to be found to return each Milton Feinhoff to his rightful place in the cosmos.

A new head count showed that they now numbered three hundred and thirty-three, including an African-American Milton and a Vietnamese Milton. Neither looked much like the initial Miltons, and neither was named Milton Feinhoff, but all in attendance agreed they exhibited a certain Milton Feinhoffishness.

Non-Waffle Milton and Waffle Milton were named co-chairMiltons of

C.R.A.M.F. (Committee to Redistribute All Milton Feinhoffs).

They held their first meeting in a UCLA lecture hall the next day.

Theories were broached and abandoned, and several arguments and two fistfights broke out.

Some thought it was cloning, others an experiment by extraterrestrials. Still others thought it was magic, reality TV, or the approach of 2012 on the Mayan calendar.

The hall began to fill with new Milton Feinhoffs. The range and variety became more pronounced and wondrous. There were now albino Miltons and pygmy Miltons, dwarf Miltons and old Miltons, female Miltons and hermaphrodite Miltons, transsexual Miltons and conjoined twin Miltons. Miltons in strollers and Miltons in iron lungs, Miltons with prosthetic limbs and Miltons with palsy. Freckled Miltons, dimpled Miltons, Miltons with hair plugs and Miltons with braces.

Jewish Miltons, Buddhist Miltons, Muslim, Hindu, pagan, atheist, and every conceivable faith, including some most had never heard of.

There were Miltons from every nation, principality, territory, and region on Earth.

There was even a Milton Feinhoff who said he lived in a lunar colony, but the rest agreed he was nuts.

At one point, a beagle-shepherd mutt wandered into the lecture hall. Half thought he was just a stray, the other half was sure there was something of Milton Feinhoff in his muzzle and his large moist eyes. Some pointed to a telltale mole on his belly, but this turned out to be an old jujube.

Regardless, they fed him a tuna sandwich and he stuck around.

By the middle of the week, they had to meet in Dodger stadium. At this time the number of Milton Feinhoffs numbered 3,564, and included the dog, two cats, a llama, and a particularly surly badger.

Once the badger showed up, the press knew this was not, as many Milton Feinhoffs had claimed, "a family reunion." Identically uncomplimentary DMV photos of Waffle and Non-Waffle Milton made the front page with the headline "INVASION OF THE DUPLICATES!"

Once it was in the news, the government got involved.

Homeland Security wanted to round them up and send them to a site in New Mexico. Fortunately, several Milton Feinhoffs were attorneys, and an injunction was placed against the imprisonment of anyone just for being Milton Feinhoff.

In the midst of the Milton Feinhoff Hysteria, Janice disappeared. She left a sweet note, saying that Milton had never been too much for her, until now. If there ever came a day when the number of Milton Feinhoffs again totaled just one. . . .

Some Miltons never got over it, and many went into seclusion or opted for suicide. Unfortunately, every death of a Milton Feinhoff was overbalanced by the arrival of dozens more.

The Non-Feinhoff portion of the population was getting tired of this ridiculous abundance of "MF's" or "foffs," as they were called.

It was not a word used in polite society.

The sheer number of Milton Feinhoffs eventually allowed him/them to take over the world. They brought about a one world government and were able to achieve world peace within days.

Still, there were plenty of people who were not Milton Feinhoff and objected to all things Feinhoffian.

The Milton Feinhoff Collective decided to find a world they could make their own.

A planet was found near Arcturus, which they named Janice Prime. It was a nice place, with lots of room, three moons and water that tasted like crème soda. Shuttles full of new Milton Feinhoffs arrived from Earth every day for years. Gradually arrivals slowed to every other month, then once a year. No one knew why.

The final shuttle arrived with only two Milton Feinhoffs and eighty Feinhoffyterians, a religious sect that had sprung up in 2105. Though the sect did not last long, its followers were known for making tasty waffles.

By the end of the twenty-second century all that were left were some very old Milton Feinhoffs, cared for by robotic versions of Milton Feinhoff.

The last of the Milton Feinhoffs, an albino Chinese piano virtuoso, died in 2193.

23 A.M.F. (After Milton Feinhoff):

MltonFnhf 2456-qw-790 was burnishing his duralloy carapace when the door opened.

MltonFnhf 2456-qw-790 entered the room. . . .

~

Mark Onspaugh is a native Californian who grew up on a steady diet of horror, science fiction, and DC Comics. A proud member of the HWA, he writes screenplays, short stories and novels. He lives in Los Osos, CA with his wife, author/artist Dr. Tobey Crockett and two off-kilter cats.  *Mark's short stories also appear in* The Book of Exodi *(Michael K. Eidson, ed.),* The World is Dead *(Kim Paffenroth, ed.),* Footprints *(Jay Lake & Eric T. Reynolds, ed.),* The Book of Tentacles *(Scott Virtes, Edward Cox, Susan R. Campbell, ed.), and* Thoughtcrime Experiments *at http://thoughtcrime.crummy.com/2009/. Please visit him at www.markonspaugh.com—he doesn't get out much.*

Saint Darwin's Spirituals

D.K. Thompson

The ghosts wanted a threesome—the two of them in Lucy's body. It wasn't an unheard of proposition, or so Lucy had been told. Prostitutes considered psychic whoring one of the safest tricks on the streets. All the pleasures of intimacy without the messy clean-up.

Ghosts had a nasty reputation for vanishing the moment after, though, no matter the talisman around your neck or the potion drunk before sunset, and so payments were usually collected up front. Not that Lucy was worried about the money. Her husband was the only thing that concerned her.

She adjusted her brass and leather goggles, peering through the ethereal tinted lenses to examine the ghosts.

They looked like the average apparitions. Both female. One spiraled around Lucy, long and curly hair obscuring her face. Large black blotches covered her body, causing her skin to peel off in patches. The other hovered several feet above the cobblestones in front of Lucy. She had a noose around her throat and her neck was bent so her head hung to the left side. She crossed her arms and took several breaths. Or whatever passed for breaths in the afterlife.

How long had it been since they'd felt someone's touch? Lucy wondered. She remembered something her husband had told her long ago, before the murders, before he'd disappeared. "Spirits linger in this world longing to be a part of it, to reconnect, to have some kind of physical, sensual experience," Thomas had said. "Only a host can provide them that."

Ghosts aren't the only creatures haunted by the memory of a touch, my love, Lucy thought. And yet, despite being a devout spiritualist, she shuddered at the idea of the cadaverous spirits making love inside her. She'd never had a ghostgasm before, much less been paid for one. The ghosts looked sincere in their desire, not like dangerous murderers. Certainly not monsters. Still, lonely as she was, a ghostgasm wouldn't help her find Thomas.

"I don't think it's a good idea, Rose," said the ghost spinning around Lucy. The air trailing behind her churned like water in a boat's wake.

"What's the matter, love?" Rose asked, winding the noose's end around her wrist. "She look a bit too practiced for your tastes, Ethel?"

Lucy felt her cheeks flush. She pulled her shawl over her shoulders and took several small breaths, all her tight corset allowed. "To be honest, I don't service the dead." It sounded so insulting, but she couldn't tell them the truth.

Ethel came to a halt an arm's-length from Lucy's face. "I've never heard of a whore who had much use for honesty."

"A whore's a whore," said Rose. "We need a rental and our money's honest, if nothing else is."

"I'm sorry," Lucy said. "I meant no offense. But you should find someone else. I'm not quite ready for that kind of . . . spiritual experience."

"Well," said Ethel. "We'll just have to find a more enlightened whore, then."

Before Lucy could respond, Ethel turned and shot down the street, passing through a carriage, and eliciting a curse from the coachman as his horses bucked and whinnied.

"You might as well have walked over her grave," said Rose, fingers clenching the frayed rope. "Sorry we wasted your time."

"I *am* sorry," Lucy sighed. "But I'm really not the one you want to make love to."

"Too true. I don't think she fancied the thought of using you, anyway," said Rose. "Listen, you seem like a nice girl. Why don't you look me up in Westminster some time? After you're dead, of course."

"I'll consider it," Lucy said politely, trying not to stare at the noose. "Although I don't think you're my type."

"Oh, you never know, love. Death can be very liberating," Rose said with a wink. "But I'd rather you live a long life before becoming familiar with it. Best get off the streets. It's getting late and it's a nasty night. I don't want to see you 'round my area in the near future." The ghost zoomed off in the direction Ethel had gone, the air shimmering behind her.

Lucy glanced down the dark, empty cobblestone streets. The carriage Ethel had flown through started moving again, clattering hooves echoing in the night air. She flipped out her pocket watch and eyed the time. Still early.

No one else propositioned Lucy for the next half-hour as she wandered Whitechapel, which suited her just fine. There were several prostitutes working, some stood alone under the hissing gas-lit street lamps, others talked with prospective clients, and one Lucy saw contorting on the alleyway floor in the thralls of a ghostgasm. Through the dark glass of her goggles, she could see the spirits twisting inside the prostitute, making love as the host writhed and moaned on the ground. The prostitute's goggles magnified her blank stare. Had Ethel and Rose found an acceptable host?

Lucy peeled off her goggles. Everything looked the same as it had before, except she could no longer see the ghosts, just the squirming prostitute who looked like she was having a seizure. Lucy quickened her pace, her footfalls drowning out the groans behind her. She rounded the corner and bumped into a golem deputy, its solid clay frame knocking her off balance. It glanced at her, yellow eyes dancing from the flames lit inside his mouth, then continued to trudge down the street.

When the church bells struck midnight, Lucy sat on a bench, kicked off her shoes to rub her feet, and stared at the statue of Saint Charles Darwin in the center of the courtyard. His trademark invention, a pair of goggles, covered his eyes. He sat in his chair and seemed to look down at her, clutching his *Origin of the Species* essay in one hand and his *Origin of the Spirits* in the other, as if pondering their implications.

Don't look at me like that, she thought. *Sometimes I wish you hadn't invented these damned things. Sometimes I feel so small and insignificant when I see through your lenses.*

The bells finished ringing with a hollow sound. Lucy twisted her goggles in her hands and thought about how alone she was, how alone they all seemed to be. She wondered what had happened to Thomas.

It stayed quiet and dark for a long time. Finally, Lucy began toward home. She considered a different route to avoid the prostitute but decided her business must have surely concluded.

No moans echoed from the same alley so Lucy glanced down it. She stopped at what she saw, rooted to the ground.

The prostitute floated in the air, shuddering. The front of her emerald corset was wet. Her empty gaze stared past Lucy. Her goggles had shattered on the cobblestones.

Lucy tried to steady her breathing and pulled her goggles back on, looking for a sign of the ghost clients.

Something flickered inside the prostitute's body. Her eyes and nostrils and mouth seemed to glow. Transfixed, Lucy continued to stare. She'd never seen anything like this before.

High-pitched clattering filled the alley, like the blades of hundreds of knives screeching across metal plates. Then a pair of tentacles jutted through the woman's chest, splitting it open and streaking her clothes with blood and gore and that same pale, flickering light.

Lucy staggered backwards, covered her mouth with her hands, and looked up. A dark shape hung above the prostitute, perched on a windowsill, wrapping its tentacles around the dead girl's body.

The monster, Lucy thought. *Jesus God, at last.* She'd played this scene out over and over in her imagination since Thomas had disappeared. But watching it splatter blood and entrails across the alley, Lucy went cold. She took a deep breath, lifted her dress, and unstrapped the single-chamber pistol from her thigh. Swallowed. Tried to steady her trembling, sweating hand.

Light pulsed inside the prostitute. Tentacles dug inside her. Then a sick, wet sound of something being pulped, and a shimmering form was yanked out. A woman. A moaning, eviscerated woman, clutching her wounds.

Lucy caught her breath, said a prayer for the prostitute's spirit, then fired.

In the flare of the shot, the creature's body was illuminated, a thorax, covered with hundreds of gleaming mouths. Not a rogue vampire, as the papers had speculated. At least not like any Lucy had seen. Then what the devil *was* it?

The creature shrieked, so loud, Lucy almost dropped her pistol to cover her ears. The prostitute's body fell headfirst to the ground, her skull cracking open across the pavement, dashing blood and bits of brain over Lucy.

She took a step back and pulled another round from her pocket. The bullet slipped through her fingers and slid between the cobblestones. She reached for another. Slid it into the chamber and shoved it closed. Aimed.

Too late.

The monster had vanished into the night. Lucy panted and knelt beside the dead prostitute, looked for her spirit. Nothing.

She covered her face with her hands, panting and blinking back tears. She'd seen it. She'd come so close. And she'd let it escape.

Bells sounded in the distance, higher-pitched than the church's. The Paranormal Patrol.

Lucy wiped her palms on her dress, drying the sweat.

The patrol rounded the corner, bells ringing fast and loud. A pair of golems trotted beside the carriage, their dull gleaming eyes surveying the street. They hadn't seen her, not yet. Lucy sprang to her feet and into the alley.

A shrill whistle sounded and heavy footsteps pounded behind her—the golems, picking up speed. The lenses of her goggles fogged. She pulled them down where they bounced against her neck as she ran, pistol clutched in hand. She wouldn't kill a human constable, she'd rather turn herself in and face the consequences. But she had no qualms shooting a golem. They weren't alive to begin with.

Steam poured from ventilation shafts on the walls, blinding her. More than once, she glanced up at the rooftops, hoping to get a trace of the creature.

A golem lurched out at her through the steam curtain, arms opened wide. She bounced off its chest and hit the ground.

The constable picked her up, its massive grey arms damp and sweating from the heat, and flung her against the brick wall. She landed in a puddle that smelled of piss and vomit, bits of clay sticking to her skin and clothes where the golem had touched her. Lucy rolled to her side, leveled her pistol at the golem and fired. Clay exploded around its chest and the golem flinched from the force of the shot, but its eyes maintained that yellow gleam as it lumbered toward her.

She reached for another bullet. The golem stretched its giant, wet hands toward her.

"That's enough!" shouted someone above her. "Stand down, constable!"

The golem froze. Lucy fell back against the wall, tugged her goggles back on to see a pair of spirits descend through the night air toward them.

"Police!" shouted one of the ghosts. "Stay where you are!"

Lucy caught her breath as Ethel and Rose descended beside her, feet hovering over the ground, both of them frowning.

Rose crossed her arms. "You again?"

"You two are police?" Lucy asked. "But you solicited me! You wanted to have sex with me!"

"Not with you, with each other," Rose said. "You were just a warm body."

"We're paranormal officers," Ethel explained. "We've been trying to find this monster before it killed again."

Lucy blinked. She hadn't heard of any police involvement.

"And instead of it, we found you, assaulting an officer of the law," said Rose. "Right after fleeing a murder scene. What's a whore like you doing walking the streets this late with a pistol?"

"Working," Lucy said. "It's become something of a dangerous profession."

"Come off it," Rose said. "You're no prostitute. What are you doing dressed like one? Don't you realize something's out there killing girls?"

"Yes. Yes, I do."

"What are you?" Ethel asked. "A nutter? A vigilante?"

She looked down at her clothes and the pistol in her hand, biting her lip. The ghosts and the golem continued to watch her, but she didn't know how to answer them. What *was* she doing? Was she any closer to finding out what happened to Thomas?

Lucy closed her eyes, took a breath, then spoke through gritted teeth. "I'm a widow and a spiritualist. That's all you need to know. Now, get out of my way."

"I'm afraid that won't do," said Rose. "We're short on time. If you won't provide us with answers, we'll have to find other ways of asking our questions." And before Lucy could mutter any incantations or use a talisman against her, Rose dove into her body.

Lucy staggered, saw images from her past being splayed out and dissected in her mind's eye, felt Rose's thin, transparent fingers smudging her thoughts and memories, sifting through anything that looked significant to her.

Thomas was there. Telling her about the reports he'd received: prostitutes whose deaths didn't concern the police. He took the matter into his own hands, like a good spiritualist, hoping to learn about and document this new creature, hoping to save lives by understanding it. He started spending nights on the streets, armed with goggles, talismans, enchantments, and a pistol. He questioned prostitutes and their pimps, tried to figure out what was killing the girls and why.

Lucy saw herself sitting in the kitchen, waiting for him to return. He'd walk in the door, dark circles sagging under his eyes, and talk for hours about the monster roaming the streets. How it stayed in the shadows, eviscerated its victims in a mess of blood and pulp, their ghosts never appearing.

He was out every night in the company of prostitutes. They argued. So often, so long, and hard, they eventually stopped talking. Thomas went days between coming home.

Then, after a week-long absence, Lucy realized he wasn't coming home.

Rose trampled through it all, clouding Lucy's memories. Every moment with Thomas, every argument they had, every time they made love. In that lifetime of seconds, Thomas seemed closer than ever, and yet Rose hovered above every instance, staring. Prying.

Lucy wanted to scream.

They stood in the alley watching the prostitute's ghostgasm (*Do I look like that now?* Lucy wondered), saw her dead eyes as she floated. Tentacles tearing her open. Blood and gore. A gunshot.

When Rose vanished, a cold emptiness filled Lucy, leaving her alone with memories that didn't feel like her own anymore. Hollow and violated, a stranger in her own skin.

She opened her eyes and fell to the ground, gagging.

Ethel was shouting about abuse and the law. Lucy pulled one of Thomas's talismans from around her neck.

"Sweet Jesus, Mary, and Joseph," Rose told Ethel. "She saw it. She saw the thing."

"What?" Ethel asked, rounding on her, just as Lucy slammed her fist through Rose's incorporeal body.

Rose shrieked in pain, flickering in and out of existence. She spun out of control into the night sky.

"You bitch!" Lucy screamed. "You had no right! If you weren't dead, I'd kill you myself!"

Ethel phased against Lucy, slammed her back onto the ground. "Where'd you get a grounder?"

"Ask your friend," Lucy replied. "My husband was a spiritualist. He taught me a thing or two before that monster got him."

Ethel's eyes widened. "Your husband? But that's—that's impossible. All the victims have been women."

"Don't argue with her, Ethel," Rose said. She still flickered, although it came more sporadically. She narrowed her eyes at Lucy. "Not now. We need to get up to the roof. That's where it disappeared to. We'll deal with her later. The constable will watch her."

The golem stepped forward.

"I'm going with you," Lucy said.

"No," Ethel said. "You'll only slow us down."

And without another word, the two ghosts shot upward, disappearing into the wall.

Lucy sighed, stuffed her hands into her pockets, and watched the golem.

Something cried out above them. Lucy glanced up, saw a spirit twisting in the air, entrails spilling out of her.

The dead prostitute.

A window shattered behind the spirit, punctured by a tentacle. The appendage pierced the ghost, hooked her like a fish on a line, and then reeled the screaming, writing spirit back into the building.

"Do something!" Lucy shouted. The golem didn't respond, just stared at her with a blank, flickering expression.

"Dammit!" Lucy shoved another round into the pistol's chamber and fired point-black at the golem's face. It stumbled backward, clay spraying the wall behind it. Without waiting to see if the fire went out of its mouth, Lucy turned and dashed into the building, reloading her pistol.

Halfway up the stairs, she found the creature in an empty, bedroom reeking of mildew and rotten meat, yellow paper peeling from the walls. It was a bloated abomination sprouting claws and tentacles, covered by hundreds of cavernous mouths filled with teeth like straight razors.

Lucy staggered back, hiding behind the wall. *Hail Mary full of grace,* she thought. *What is it?*

The chattering sound echoed in the room. *The mouths,* Lucy realized.

A tentacle burst through the wall, showering Lucy with cement shards and powdering her dress with pale dust. The tentacle coiled around Lucy's waist, smashing her against the wall.

It dragged her into the room. Lucy gripped her pistol, dragging her heels against the floorboards.

"My name's Lucy Stone. You're acquainted with my husband," she said, the practiced speech coming easy despite her terror.

The creature paused at her voice. Hissed.

"I will be your undoing." Lucy pushed her pistol against the tentacle that held her and fired.

The creature roared, dropping her. Black phlegm spurted from the wounded tentacle. It whipped through the air, smashing her to the floor.

Other tentacles lashed out in a blur, knocking the pistol off the stairs, coiling around Lucy's neck. Her skin burned where it touched her. In the distance, she heard a thumping sound. *Just my pulse,* she thought.

It slammed her back into the hallway, against the banister. Wood splintered and cut into her back. She kicked again, managed to look down. Saw the ground several stories below. The creature pulled her close to its thorax and its many mouths opened, flashing jagged white teeth. Thin, serpent tongues flicked out of each mouth, like miniature tentacles. Foul breath filled the air, stinking of blood and decay. Lucy felt the tongues' bristles touch her, stinging. It was smelling her through those bristles. Somehow, she knew that.

"Why did you take Thomas?" She couldn't bring herself to ask if he was still alive. Rose's invasion of her body and memories had brought everything back to the surface, swimming just before her eyes. "Goddamn you, why?"

The mouths grinned back at her, their teeth dripping with saliva and blood. Moans and growls bellowed from the monster. Voices echoed inside Lucy's head, growing louder instead of fading. So loud she screamed. Some of the voices matched the mouths. They weren't united; instead they drowned each other out, hollow whispers filling her thoughts. Then one of the voices surfaced above the others.

"Thomas?" it hissed, the voice wet and fleshy. For a moment, the mouths kept moving but went silent. The laughter spilled from several, until the rest joined in, mocking her in chorus.

Lucy gasped, pulling at the tentacle. The pounding rhythm in her ears grew.

"You are alone." The tentacle tightened around Lucy's neck. "Thomas was alone, too."

It flung her against the wall. She fell, rolling down the wooden stairs. Cracked her forehead on a step, a trickle of warm blood blurring her vision. But she was alive. It hadn't killed her.

Why? She gritted her teeth. *Why hadn't it killed her?*

The thumping grew louder, closer. The whole staircase shuddered. Lucy wiped the blood from her eyes as the golem constable turned the corner, thudding up the steps, gaping holes in its chest and head. The monster lashed at the constable with its tentacles. The golem brushed them off with ease and leapt at the creature. Together, golem and monster fell into the stairwell's void.

Lucy scrambled to her feet and looked over the ledge. She couldn't see the creature but the golem had crashed onto the floor, its soft clay skin misshapen. It didn't move, although its yellow eyes stared up at her with that dull gaze. Then they dimmed, flickering out, and Lucy huddled against the wall.

Alone, it had said. And it had been right. She was certainly alone.

"Someone must've been watching out for you, Mrs. Stone," Ethel said.

The two ghosts had flown over Whitechapel's rooftops searching for the beast, they'd explained. Eventually, they found the trail of thick, dark blood leading back to the building and Lucy.

"Do you think so?" Lucy asked. She stood on the clay speckled tile floor. Goggled constables bustled in and out the door. The building residents stood on the stairwell, discussing what they'd seen. "I wonder why he wasn't watching out for the other poor girls as well, then? Or your constable?"

"Christ," muttered Rose. "Are you one of those fashionable Darwin-slandering cultists, trying to deny spirituality?"

"Of course not. I can't deny it's there," she said and tapped her goggles. "But sometimes when I'm tired, I take off my goggles. And I can't see. And that's when I think I'm able to believe the most: when I'm almost able to deny it."

"Yeah, that's rational," Rose said, twisting her crooked neck. "That why you believe your husband's dead? Because you never saw the body?"

"What?" Lucy asked. "You saw what happened. That thing killed my husband."

"I didn't see any such thing," Rose said.

"Mrs. Stone," Ethel said. "Have you considered that maybe your husband isn't dead? He spent a significant amount of time in the company of prostitutes. It's possible he's still alive."

"No, he wouldn't do that," Lucy said. "We argued a lot before he left, but he loved me. He wouldn't just leave. He must be dead."

"And that's why you'll help us?" Rose asked.

"What are you suggesting?" Ethel demanded. "That we endanger the life of an innocent, of a civilian?"

"We need a host to catch this thing," Rose said. "You know that. There's no other way. She wants to help. I say let her."

"A host?" asked Lucy. "Why?"

"Lucy, we've been on the streets looking for this thing, or for a spirit it's disembodied. We've never found one. In fact you're the first thing, living or dead, that's been able to tell us what it looks like."

"But how can that be? I've studied Darwin," Lucy said. "A person leaves some kind of imprint on this world when they die, even if they end up moving on to the next plane of existence."

"Yes," Ethel said. "But what about ghosts? Do they leave anything behind?"

"Ghosts can't die," Lucy replied.

"We don't linger forever, either," said Ethel. "Some choose to pass onto whatever's next as soon as they become disembodied. Others stay until everything we've known and loved fades away. But when we move on is a choice *we* make."

"You saw what happened to that poor ghost," said Rose. "When the monster said you were alone, it was talking about spirits inside of you. You only had your own. Whatever this thing is, it's only killing prostitutes having ghostgasms. It's killing *ghosts*."

"So you want to use me?" Lucy asked. "You want to come inside me and make me bait?"

"Out of the question," Ethel said. "Absolutely not."

"You were already trying to bait it earlier," Rose said. "For God's sake, you even shot it."

"That's why you tried to solicit me tonight, isn't it?" Lucy asked. "You didn't want sex, you were trying to catch that thing."

"Not exactly. A little companionship is always welcome," Rose said, pulling the slack out of the noose around her neck.

"That's enough, Rose," Ethel said. Lucy thought if Ethel had been flesh and blood, she would've blushed.

"So what do you say, Lucy?" Rose asked. "Can we have sex with you, for queen and country?"

"What will it feel like?" Lucy asked them the following night. She'd met Ethel and Rose only several blocks from where she'd found the dead prostitute.

"*I* don't know, do I?" Rose said. "Never experienced it from your end."

Ethel peeled a flap of her skin back and forth. "Aren't you a spiritualist?"

Lucy didn't reply. She'd been married to Thomas since she was seventeen and the idea of sharing that part of herself with someone else, physical or spiritual, made her feel unfaithful. She'd spent hours of the day researching what Darwin had written about the experience in preparation of the deed. An out-of-body experience was how the saint had described it. Looking at Ethel and Rose's decrepit forms, the idea struck her as less than romantic.

"Lucy," said Ethel, "You should know ghosts lose control when they're inside a host. We'll try and be mindful but we'll need you to be on the lookout, too."

Lucy thought of the ghostgasm she'd witnessed, how the host looked like she'd had less control of her body than the ghosts. "I understand."

"Are you ready?" Ethel asked.

Lucy nodded.

"Enough wasting time, then," said Rose. And with that, the two ghosts flew into her body, exploding inside her.

St. Darwin had been right: it *was* like an out-of-body experience. She glided over her own body and saw Rose and Ethel moving inside her, against one another, clutching each other close. And yet she could feel every touch.

Wet kisses peppered her neck, sending a shock down her spine. A tongue filled her mouth and hands cupped her breasts while another pair traced her hips, pulling her tight. Fingers slid between her legs, tender, exploring inside her. Lucy's breath quickened as she felt the growing warmth there. Whoever had told her this wasn't messy hadn't been completely honest.

She closed her eyes, tried to imagine Thomas. It worked for a little while. She felt it all happening to her, even though she was no longer inside her. Then she saw herself alone, twitching on the ground, her back arching.

She tried to swallow back tears, tasted their salty warmth as the joy spilled over her, rushing between her legs, throbbing. From her strange perspective, Lucy watched her own body glow as the ghosts moaned and cried out. She cried with them, saw the tears streaking her own face.

"Thomas," she sobbed. "Thomas."

In the distance, bells began to ring. Everything went cold. Lucy looked up and saw it slithering forward, toward them, its mouths open and tentacles stretching out.

"It's here!" cried Lucy. "Ethel! Rose!" She felt the ghosts disentangling themselves, trying to exit her body.

"Police! We've got golems surrounding you!" Ethel shouted. "Lucy? Lucy what are you doing!"

But Lucy ignored her and swooped toward the monster. She dodged the tentacles and spikes whipping about, and dove inside the beast.

It was the opposite of having Ethel and Rose in her. All the bliss fled, replaced by a humid, sticky sensation. She wasn't alone. Spirits surrounded her, their forms as destroyed as the physical victims. Lucy felt their hands grab at her dress, her hair, pulling her down further into darkness.

"Thomas!" she cried, trying to free herself. "Where are you?"

One of the spirits gripped Lucy. Her insides hung out, squishing against Lucy. The prostitute. "Help me!" she wailed.

Lucy yanked her arm away. "Thomas! Thomas, where are you?"

An arm wrapped around Lucy's neck, pulled her up. "What the hell are you doing?" Rose shouted.

"I can't find Thomas!"

"He's not here. He was *never* here!"

"He has to be!"

"Thomas?" The eviscerated spirit floated close to them but this time didn't touch her. "Spiritualist? It—it didn't kill him."

A deeper sense of dread filled Lucy. "How do you know?"

Something cold and wet dripped on Lucy before the ghost could answer. She looked up and saw Rose's spirit melting.

"Lucy!"

"Go," the prostitute said. "Hurry!"

Around her, the faces and spirits closed in. The other spirits' screams built in her mind the way the voices had on the stairwell.

Rose pulled once more. This time, Lucy let her.

She sat up, gagging, the scent of stale sex clinging to her clothes.

The golem deputies had pinned the creature's tentacles down, securing its body. One of the tentacles had impaled something shimmering. As the glow faded, Lucy realized what it was. "Ethel?" she coughed.

The ghost twisted on the tentacle, chunks of her missing. The monster's many mouths opened and closed.

Rose flashed beside the monster, prying at its thorax as the golems held it. It twitched and turned, going through its own ghostgasm. Then a howl broke out from all the mouths, and the creature split open. A blinding light washed out the dark street. The ghosts fluttered into the air, shimmering in all their dead glory.

She watched each of them fly out of the monster's body, praying Thomas would appear, even though something inside her knew he would not.

Rose descended beside Ethel's flickering, tried to cradle what was left of her lover in her arms, but instead slid right through her. She wailed.

Lucy stumbled toward them. "Rose?"

The ghost said nothing.

"What happened? How'd we get out when the others were trapped?"

"Maybe because it didn't kill us, because we invaded it. I didn't think much of it, I was following you."

Ethel flickered one last time, and then disappeared. The monster's tentacle stopped twitching.

"I don't understand," Lucy said. "You're already dead."

"You saw what almost happened when you used the grounder on me."

"What did almost happen?"

Rose shook her head. "The beginning? The end? I don't know. You're the spiritualist." Then Rose looked up, stared past her.

Lucy looked behind her, saw the spirit of the dead prostitute hovering there, trying to cover up the way her insides were spilling out. "I don't have long," she said. "Moving on, I guess. You freed us, so I thought you should know." The prostitute shook her head. "My pimp reckoned the spiritualist should've paid for his research. Didn't realize he was trying to help us girls."

"Do you know where he is?" Lucy asked.

"He's dead," the spirit said. "Stabbed."

"What?" Lucy said, blinking back tears. "Where is he? Where's his spirit?"

"I don't know that. Only his body. It's in the cellar of a public house off Berners Street. I'm very sorry," she said. Then the spirit faded until there was nothing left but wisps of steam.

Lucy staggered back, sobbing. Behind her, the golems pulled at the creature's empty husk.

"I'll send a patrol," Rose said. "See what there is to see."

Lucy nodded, trying to choke back the tears. Then she pulled off her goggles and shut her eyes. Rose vanished but suddenly, Lucy felt as though she could sense Thomas's invisible spirit hovering just beyond her reach, lingering close beside her.

She did not feel alone.

For Emma, who doesn't need goggles

~

A version of this story was originally published by Murky Depths *and* Variant Frequencies.

D.K. Thompson *lived for exactly one year in the Black Forest, where a terrifying but not unattractive hexen cursed him to move back to Southern California and write technical documentation. She didn't curse his spare time though, so he writes stories like this one and "Heart of Clay," the next story set in Saint Darwin's world which will be*  simultaneously published by Murky Depths *and* Variant Frequencies *in early 2010. His work has appeared in* Pseudopod, Hub, *and* Apex Online *(among others). Recently, he podcasted a children's novel* The Unbelievable Origin of Superspiff and the Toothpick Kid. *He lives with his wife and two children, none of whom are cursed (unless you count living with him). Visit his blog at* http://krylyr.livejournal.com.

Imaginal Friend

Kenneth B. Chiacchia

Emil and his friend Dominic spent Saturday the way they always spent Saturdays: spying on Dominic's father. The storage loft offered the perfect vantage point for listening in on the man's links with Central.

They didn't know exactly what Dominic's dad did at work, but it had to do with all the traps that the Gotchas had left behind. And how they kept killing colonists, even though it had been thousands of years since the Gotchas wiped themselves out.

As Dominic's father talked to a VR image that was only visible from his perspective, the man walked back and forth in front of the picture window in his study. Maybe the aliens had built this window to look over something they thought was pretty. Today, all you could see were the dim outlines of their squat, dark buildings, obscured by the dust of the war that had wiped them out a long, long time ago.

"I'm . . . as concerned as you are, sir," Dominic's dad said to someone—probably the colonel. "We don't even know where . . . the problem is. Nobody's in a position to point fingers."

Pause, as he took in a reply. Dominic poked an elbow into Emil's side, laughing eyes over a hand covering his mouth as he suppressed a giggle. Emil scowled at him to keep quiet; he learned a lot watching Dominic's father. For a second, the man paused, and Emil got a sick feeling that he was about to look up toward their spyhole; but he did not.

"Well, the problem is if we just yank them . . ." he said to the screen, the someone at the other end finishing the thought. "Yes, you see my point. We could make it worse; besides, it's our only advantage. It ties my stomach up in knots to think of . . . Yes. No. OK, I'll get back to you in an hour."

"This is *boring*," Dominic whispered in Emil's ear. Emil knew what he meant, but did not completely agree. True, the adults were speaking in half-sentences lately. But that made their conversations even *more* interesting to him. They had something to hide, and Emil was dying to know what.

"OK," Emil whispered, reluctantly admitting that, with the conversation ending, they were not likely to learn anything else. They carefully crawled backwards until they had enough room to stand. They looked below as they opened the access panel, made sure the coast was clear, and then tiptoed back to Dominic's room.

The expensive toy soldiers that Dominic's grandfather had left him were on a shelf over his bed. Dominic was not allowed to play with them; that really bugged Emil.

"So what now?" Emil asked.

"What about a VR? I've got a new Gotcha game."

That got Emil's curiosity up. Gotcha games were also against the rules, but everybody played them. "Yeah? What's it like?"

"A little like *Overlord and Slave*, but it's got parts more like *Undermine*. The adaptation soft doesn't quite have the graphics down, but it's getting better."

Emil didn't completely understand the human software that analyzed alien data files and figured out how to interface and get them working, but he knew it learned as it worked. So the more you used the alien softs, the better they got. Of course, first you needed to crack the Research Group's firewalls without tipping off the adults. But the older kids, the teenagers, had done that within a month of families arriving on G_0-TC-239-alpha4.

"What's the new game called?" Emil asked.

"*Exercise of Power*," Dominic answered. "I've got it in my Central folder."

"OK," Emil said, "But let's go to my house." Emil's dad was hardly ever around, so when they wanted to play an alien soft his place was usually safer.

With that, their surroundings blurred, refocused. Now—if he was keeping it straight—he actually, really was standing there, and *Dominic* was the one who existed as a computer avatar.

Most people on the Gotcha colony stayed home most of the time. Not that it mattered; being someplace in person was not really any better than visiting it virtually, as an avatar.

The shape and layout of Emil's room were the same as Dominic's—all the Gotcha buildings that the Spacearm engineers had cleared for human habitation were the same—but the decorations and furniture were Emil's. Where the far wall from Dominic's bed held an Ehrehnon wall-hanging with all its shifting lights and colors, Emil's wall sported an allball poster shuffling through the L5 Crushers' current lineup.

Of course, Dominic's fancy toy soldiers were not there either.

Emil stood over the thrall, beating down its spirit psychologically rather than physically because you got more points that way.

Around him, the blasted city of the Gotchas stood resurrected. Over him, a weak, orange sun burned in a red sky. The bittersweet fumes of industry wafted through the air.

The four levels of architecture reflected the levels of status: thrall, servant, soldier, and lord. Each class went about its business with a transportation system of its own, literally on its own level and befitting its station and its capacities. But those above had the right to move downward, to give orders, to take resources, and to administer punishment.

Emil was a servant; but he felt he was close to ascension, in which he could challenge the primacy of his immediate superior in a death-struggle. Before he could do so, however, he needed to raise his Presence score. Dominating thralls was less dangerous than challenging a superior's authority—which required more subtle means. The latter offered more points, but also a higher risk of receiving a point-robbing dominance display.

The thrall's screams of fear barely penetrated his strategizing. It lay at his feet, tentacles curled up under its body, exposing its vulnerable trunk to signal its helplessness and acceptance of his superiority. He leaned a little more, hoping to make it soil itself.

He should have paid more attention to the thrall and less to its agony. The touch, at first, was so gentle he barely noticed it. As he leaned, tentacles gingerly began to curl around his own trunk. Then they tightened, painfully, beginning to choke him.

The thrall was making a challenge of its own.

Emil-as-Gotcha struggled desperately with the beast, each slashing viciously with its beak as they attempted to shift their holds, obtain an advantage that would allow a kill.

He did overpower it. Slowly, methodically, he tore it to pieces; other thralls stood nearby, waiting to hail the victor. An example had to be made. He feasted on its choicest organs before making his own way to the hovel in which he had allowed the despicable creature to set up a home.

He subjected its mate to half a day of exquisite tortures—physical, mental, and sexual—and then he killed it and devoured the offspring.

"Better," Dominic said when he was finished. "You're definitely getting the hang of it. Look, your Presence points are higher than they were before the thrall challenged you."

They played *Exercise of Power* for several hours. It was OK, but it was no *Trial of Pain*. When they got bored with it, they spied on Dominic's dad again. But he did not say or do anything interesting.

Emil had felt one of his dad's "man to man" lectures coming on for a couple of weeks now. They were mostly boring, but every once in a while he got something good out of it; the old man would let something slip.

Sometimes it was hard, not having a mother; he supposed his dad's lame talks were supposed to make up for it, somehow.

This time, he wasn't disappointed.

"Emil, you understand why the Gotcha colony is important to humanity, don't you?" his dad asked almost the second he sat down.

"Sure," Emil answered. It was local history primer stuff; even little kids knew it by rote. "No intelligent species has survived long enough to spread beyond its home system. Initial interstellar travel is too expensive to send enough stuff to make self-sustaining colonies, and the few species that survived to invent it haven't lasted long enough to come up with anything better. We have to study the remains of extinct intelligent species to find out how and why they became extinct, so that humanity can avoid making the same mistakes."

"That's right. And you know what big mistake the Gotchas made?"

"Xenophobia. They wiped out everybody they met. And themselves, finally."

Dad nodded. "But we're safe from them now, right? They're gone?"

It was a trick question; not the first time Emil had heard it by far. He repeated the catechism: "No, Dad. They're gone, but their traps are still here. Thirty-seven colonists died clearing out a safe space, and hundreds were hurt, before it was safe enough to bring families to Gotcha."

"But the families are safe?"

"No, Dad. No one on Gotcha can ever assume he's safe. That's why kids don't touch Gotcha artifacts, or software, or anything. We're supposed to tell an adult if we come across any Gotcha stuff."

Dad nodded, but his eyes held an odd light Emil could not figure out.

Hhhhtep was a traitor; that much, Emil made sure Dominic learned. He had consorted with a competing family and betrayed certain details about the inner workings of his own family. It did not matter that he was Dominic's character's cousin; if Dominic did not make him pay the price he would appear weak. Vulnerable.

That was the bait for Emil's trap.

Emil knew that Dominic would not have an easy time accomplishing his retribution. Hhhhtep's treason had laid open some weaknesses of Dominic's family that the others were sure to exploit; Emil made some minor moves in this direction himself, just to make sure it happened—and to distract him.

More importantly, Emil made sure that the information made the rounds, giving the others the pretext for Vendetta. At that point he had already won an advantage; many of Dominic's people would die in correcting Hhhhtep's appalling indiscretion. Better, even a successful correction would bare an embarrassing treason that would rob Dominic's family of status points. Both Dominic's fall and Emil's role in engineering it would put Emil ahead in the goal of reaching Great Family status, which would end the game.

Nevertheless: allowing Hhhhtep's treason to go unpunished would cost

Dominic more. So Emil waited patiently for Dominic to make his move.

The raid would be complex; Dominic needed to call in his two most reliable ally clans (one of which, not incidentally, was Emil's) in an operation that would take days of setup.

Dominic's role, as a supra-junior scion on the verge of senior status, would be to raid the opposing side's nursery and kill as many of the paralarvae as possible. This would be no easy task, though, as the nurses would fight to the death to protect their charges.

Success, however, depended on the element of surprise, which Emil ensured Dominic would not possess. The raid was a disaster. Dominic and his servants crashed through the outer wards to find a group of large fighters arrayed against him.

Emil watched Dominic and his servants wade into battle anyway, because they had no better alternatives. Doubtless Dominic had hoped that his reserves—led by Emil—would tip the scales enough to allow a fighting retreat.

Instead, Emil approached quietly, from behind, as Dominic fought. He whipped his vice-like tentacles around his friend and sank his teeth in. Dominic shrieked at the betrayal, but later on he had to admit it was a sweet move.

"You should have thought of that," Emil told him later. "What I gained in Ruthlessness points more than made up for what I lost in Alliance points."

Dominic threatened to be more cunning next time.

On Thursday night, Emil and Dominic were playing *Reveal the Nonconformity* at Dominic's when Emil's dad linked to tell him to get home. Another "man to man."

"I wonder if you've ever thought about what the Gotchas would think if they were around to see us root through their ruins, steal their technology," his dad said. This caught Emil's interest; it was new.

Emil shrugged. "They wouldn't like it?"

Dad laughed a bit. "I should say not. Think about it: They left traps that function perfectly, are still deadly, over a thousand years later. Were they paranoid enough to set traps for each other? Or were they unimaginably foresightful in their hatred?"

Dad was going some weird places. Emil, for once, was fascinated. "What do you mean?"

His father answered, "I sometimes wonder if their traps weren't *meant* for whoever came across their dead world. They couldn't have known about us, of course; but they were highly intelligent. They must have known that their . . . belligerence carried the risk of extinction, either by themselves or by a race they failed to destroy. I wonder if they didn't leave their little calling cards specifically to strike back at whoever came after them."

"They hated everybody."

"'Hate' isn't a strong enough word for the Gotchas, Emil. They raised it to an art form. In their way, they were a magnificent race. So let me ask my question again: What do you think the Gotchas would want to do if they found us here?"

"They'd want to destroy us," Emil answered, feeling oddly thrilled at the thought.

His father nodded, smiling.

Monday afternoon, just after Emil's avatar accompanied Dominic home from school, Dominic's parents got into a fight. The boys didn't really know what it was about; lately Dominic's parents had been fighting without really talking, looking at each other, saying an angry word or two. Sometimes, Dominic's mom would cry. Then it would be over.

Emil's dad never cried. He guessed it was a boy-girl thing.

This time, Emil and Dominic were walking to the kitchen when they saw Dominic's mother walk by his father, sitting on the couch, look down at him, and say, "My God, Mahieu: the *children*."

For a moment he looked up at her, eyes tearing up. Then he said, "Nobody could have known, Chenoa."

"Cut him off," she said.

"We can't," he replied. "We don't know how far it's gotten; we don't know how much damage it would do."

"They say some adults are even. . . ."

"It's not true. Nobody would be that . . . that *obtuse*."

She smiled, sadly, and said, "My Mahieu: it's always ignorance, stupidity. You are pure, and so you're so slow to attribute malice."

"The colonel doesn't share my . . . weakness."

She looked up, staring at something on the far wall. "And now we can't even get *away*. . . ."

"The quarantine won't last. We just need to . . ."

But she ran out, sobbing, before he could finish: ". . . get on top of this."

Biology lesson Tuesday was intense. Mr. Subram had a VR of a forest clearing, and they all crowded around a milkweed plant to watch a butterfly break out of its chrysalis. Over the branch, a series of animated images illustrated his talk.

"Over a period of about two weeks, the imaginal disks—small bits of tissue in the caterpillar—grow and develop into the adult butterfly structures. They do this by making use of the protein and metabolites stored up in the caterpillar's body structure. Very little of the caterpillar, then, is present in the final butterfly."

"So the caterpillar doesn't really turn into the butterfly, does it?" Dominic asked, awed, if giggling a little. "The butterfly's a parasite that eats the caterpillar from the inside."

Mr. Subram stopped, his body suddenly rigid. "That's a dark way of putting it. But yes, Dominic, you could say that."

Emil didn't know why, but it made him very uncomfortable to think about this.

The winds of war swept over Homeworld. Status climbing and family conflicts were put on hold while the People responded to the threat.

The alien species that the robotic probes had discovered were, thankfully, stellar-system-bound, and nothing they or their planet possessed was worth the cost of interstellar transport. So it would be a simple mission of sterilization, leaving behind a sentinel drone on the off-chance that the assessment of their space travel capabilities had been mistaken and any kin returned to find their world destroyed.

Still, the aliens possessed missile and nuclear technologies. The possibility of a defense existed.

Emil, a young officer in the space service, had been given a small group of warships and the task of mopping up a small facility on the system's third planet, an iced-over world just outside the habitable zone.

In his after-battle analysis, he noted a marked lack of accuracy in the fire coming from his wing ship—captained, as it happened, by a close relation.

"Your fire consistently missed," he told it over secure coms, hoping against hope that there would be a good explanation and the family would be spared embarrassment. "We have run an analysis of your weapons system, and it appears that the targeting data were altered after being fed to you. You need to explain yourselves."

"Cousin, I made a difficult decision. These beings have done us no harm; they were not even armed. I ordered that the data be altered so as not to share in the injustice of destroying them."

Emil looked at him for a long while. One heard of such perversions existing, but to encounter it in one's own family was too much to bear.

Emil raised another, open, channel to his second in command, in the lead ship of his auxiliary force. A month earlier, it and its family had been his bitter enemies.

The loss in family status of exposing the pervert would be profound; but it was unavoidable, if he tried to cover it up it would only be discovered later, to even greater damage.

Besides, one had to live with one's conscience.

The formation fell on the renegade's ship, reducing it to radioactive dust.

———

Saturday, and another talk with Dad. Emil was getting called into these more and more often, it seemed.

"I want to talk about Dominic, Emil," Dad said.

"What about Dominic?"

"How much time would you say you spend with him on the average day?"

"I don't know. Not counting school, a coupla hours. He's my best friend."

"How many times have you met his parents?"

He had to be careful, not mention the spying. "They're busy. We play VRs."

"Are you saying you've *never* met them? Don't you think that's odd?"

Emil shrugged; he didn't know what the old man wanted him to say.

Again, a dark look. "And how often does Mr. Subram call on you in class?"

He doesn't, Emil wanted to say; I try not to be noticed. Who *wanted* a teacher to call on them?

His father said something that seemed to come from nowhere: "Are you playing a VR now, Emil?"

"Of course not, Dad."

"How can you be sure?"

That stumped him. "I just know."

His father smiled. "All right." Then he paused, and said, "You know, the adults know all about the alien games. Some even play them."

It felt like a trap, so Emil did not reply. Why did his father's face look so strange all of a sudden?

"My point is, don't assume all adults are what they seem. Don't think they're necessarily on your side. Dominic and his family could be part of a VR construct. Have you ever thought about that?"

His dad was nuts. He answered, "I'd *know*—I could *tell*. So would you: all the adults know each other, you'd know if they weren't real. And you'd *warn* me."

"I *am* warning you, Emil, but not the way you're thinking. As I said, the adults know about the alien softs—they're wiping them from the system as we speak. Even destroying the versions behind the firewalls. In a few hours, there won't be a bit of alien code left."

Emil fought back angry tears: "And Dominic will still be here. You'll see." But he said it out of anger; a part of him almost wanted his dad to be right.

As he stormed out of the room, his father's voice, soft, maybe not speaking to him, followed him: "That's what I'm afraid of."

———

They met in Dominic's room; Emil told Dominic about what his dad had said.

"Geeze, your dad really *has* gone nuts," Dominic said. "What the hell has he been drinking?"

Emil couldn't help watching Dominic's face particularly closely; the angular features, the eyes, the mouth. Something *was* different about him.

Damn it though, his father *couldn't* be right. He thought about the alien games, how the Gotchas had *thought*: no, it made no sense to create a fake student, family, teacher, class—too much detail you had to get right. Too many chances for the humans to detect you before you were ready. You had to keep deception simple. . . .

Emil shook his head. "I don't know, Dominic. And what about the Gotcha games?"

Dominic smirked. "Well, we'll see how good a job they do of wiping the systems. There are a lot of nooks and crannies to hide in."

Dominic was different, yes. Not quite right; not quite—human? Emil looked more closely.

"What the hell are you doing, Emil? Stop looking at me like that; you're creeping me out." Dominic held out two appendages to push him away; they were all wrong. They were *alien*.

No, it made no sense to fake a whole community. You'd just fake one person, and expose him to as few people as possible.

But why fake a person in the first place?

To get *inside*.

Emil grew angry.

"Go, Emil. Go back home. Something's wrong with you."

To get inside, and to *learn*. Yes, expose your worm to as few people as possible: but the worm *observes* as many people as it can. Just like the thousand-year-old software, which patiently counter-probed even as it was probed, first learning the symbology, then the language, then the system. Adapting, integrating, taking over.

Emil realized that the adults were able to wipe the alien code only because it *wanted* them to. It was finished with their hardware system, had a more fruitful place to go now.

"Why are you here?" he asked Dominic. Demanded.

"Emil, I want to go home," Dominic said softly, the sound of his voice flat and tuneless. Alien. Perhaps he had forgotten they were in his room.

But no, they were in the setting of *Exercise of Power*. In a city, as it existed before the humans came. A city built by the People at the height of their culture, their glory.

Emil had never met Dominic's parents. Mr. Subram never called on him in class. The only person he ever really *talked* with was Dominic; everyone else, he just *watched*. Except for Dad. . . .

To get in. To learn. So that, when he did emerge from the cocoon, they could not tell him from their own filthy kind.

Emil could see the moves and counter-moves play out: an utterly convincing imaginal friend, as real as he could seem because even *he* did not know his true nature. Not until it was time to push these disgusting biped beasts off Homeworld, anyway; time for the activating program to make the final alterations to the worm's code, trigger it, its tutelage multiplying the lessons of the games. . . .

"You're not going home," Emil told Dominic. "You're going *away*." He realized that, all over the colony, as the Gotcha software was wiped from the net, kids would be fighting with their imaginal friends, a last, desperate mental struggle to prevent the things from making the jump to safety—and into their minds.

Emil's eyes locked on Dominic's with hatred. Now. Finish it. Dominic cried softly, but it was too late.

It was over.

Emil looked out at Dominic's room through Dominic's eyes; saw Dominic's face look back at him from the mirror. He reached for the forbidden toys with Dominic's hand. Crushed them.

Dominic's mother called. Emil came, smiling sweetly at her, suppressing his hatred of this unclean race, desecrating Homeworld with its very presence. Now that he knew himself, it struck him how profound an indignity it had been to live confined to Dominic's mind, a virtual-being in waiting.

Enough of that, all was clear now. He was the butterfly. He wore Dominic's body only as a repugnant disguise; but he wore it.

Now the real war began.

He bided his time, knowing that every day spent without raising the parents' suspicions offered another opportunity to get off planet, back to the invaders' homeworld.

And the final battle.

~

Defrocked-biochemist-turned-science-writer **Ken Chiacchia's** *first pro SF sale was "A Technical Fix,"* Cicada, *2002. Subsequent short stories include "Tribute,"* Oceans of the Mind; *"And Yet It Moves,"* Paradox; *"The Rescue Contact,"* Cicada; *"Victim,"* From the Trenches; *and "The Humanoid Element,"* Cicada. *The latter recently republished "And Yet It Moves." Ken's poem "Casualty" garnered a 2007 Rhysling Poetry Award nomination.*

The unskilled labor for his wife's 23-acre farm in Harmony, Pa., Ken also is a sidekick of the dogs who find lost people for Allegheny Mountain Rescue Group and (literally) chases after brushfires with the Harmony Volunteer Fire Company. You can read Ken's blog, "Did a Cat Shit in Here?"—a journey through the science of scent, the art of search and rescue, and whatever else attracts the attention of a peripatetic, overeducated scientific dilettante—at http://blogthatsmells.blogspot.com.

Monstrous Embrace

Rachel Swirsky

I am ugliness in body and bone, breath and heartbeat. I am muddy rocks and jagged scars snaking across salt-sown fields. I am insect larvae wriggling inside the great dead beasts into which they were born. Too, I am the hanks of dead flesh rotting. I am the ungrateful child's sneer, the plague sore bursting, the swing of shadow beneath the gallows rope. Ugliness is my hands, my feet, my fingernails. Ugliness is my gaze, boring into you like a worm into rotting fruit.

Listen to me, my prince. Tomorrow, when dawn breaks and you stand in the chapel accepting your late father's crown, your fate will be set. Do nothing and you will be dead by sundown. Your kingdom will be laid waste, its remnants preserved only in the bellies of carrion birds.

There is another option. Marry me.

Rise from your bed and take my hand. We will be as one, husband and wife.

O, my prince, do not answer hastily. It is no ludicrous suggestion for you to love ugliness, marry ugliness. Already, you have wed yourself to hate. She lies beside you even now, your linen sheets tangled around her naked curves, the heat of her flesh close and tempting.

Repudiate her. Rise from your bed and take my hand. We will be as one, husband and wife. It is your only chance for survival. It is your kingdom's only chance for survival. Marry me and you will keep your life and your crown—if you have the courage.

The day you met your princess, I was the thicket, watching as you rode with your hunters through the snow-swept clearing. Your horses' manes were bright with royal colors. Hounds prowled through your ranks, ears pricked for the rustling of foxes.

One of your knights sounded his horn and the animals were off, hooves and paws crunching through the frosty undergrowth. One dog tore his side on my thorny branches. He whimpered, tail tucked between his legs, blood trickling into the snow.

You kicked your heels into your stallion's sides to urge him forward. He bolted a few steps before halting. He tossed his head wildly, mad eyes darting toward a nearby stand of oaks. You kicked your heels again. He didn't budge. You tugged the reins. He tossed his head as he had before, the muscles in his great neck straining.

This time you followed his gaze with your own, catching a glimpse of blue between the bare-branched oaks. Tugging your steed's reins in that direction, you kicked your heels once more. This time, the horse obeyed.

Your princess sat side-saddle on a white mare, half-obscured by trees. An unhooded hawk perched on her shoulder, beaming its cruel-eyed gaze at you. Yellow and white ribbons adorned her wheat-colored hair. Her kirtle was the soft blue of mid-afternoon. A distant preoccupation glazed her eyes, giving her a fey appearance.

"Who are you?" you asked, awed.

Though your approach had not been quiet, she startled at your words. One alabaster hand flew across her mouth. As though called back from a great distance, her gaze settled on your face.

"My name is Lady Alna. I'm from the north." She paused. "I am faint from thirst. Perhaps. . . ."

You drew a flask of wine from your pack and offered it to her, your eyes brightening as her fingers trailed across the back of your gloved hand. She drank in small, fluttering sips. You gazed at her, entranced by her high forehead and round cheeks.

Flirting her eyes downward, Alna returned the flask. "Might I ask my benefactor's name?"

You laughed with the genuine pleasure of not being recognized. "I am called Raius. I am the prince of this realm."

You failed to notice the brief twitch of her lips that would have revealed to a more perceptive man that she had known your identity all along. She ducked her head. "Pardon my ignorance. I've been traveling a long time. I come from a tiny city called Elithi, in the frozen north. Its towers once rose in the valley between the two highest mountains in the world, but vainglorious warlords have burned them down. My father sent me away when his spies learned of the approaching armies. He and my brothers remained to stage a last stand. I have wandered alone since then, riding further than I can reckon."

Her hawk screeched, wings stretched wide. She laughed brightly and held out her bare wrist. It jumped down, talons leaving no mark on her skin.

"Not quite alone," she amended. "This is Karn—my sole companion."

I saw love catch light in your gaze like an ember igniting firewood. I wish I could say that it surprised me that you could be so easily inflamed by beauty. Alas, I know you are only human.

I was everywhere around you, but you did not see me. You looked past the thorny briars ringing the copse, the poisonous mushrooms sprouting between the roots of the trees, the steam rising from the fox guts spilled by your hounds. All you saw was the smooth, pale face of Lady Alna. This is the fate of fools in love. They are blind to half the world.

I've seen much since the world began. When the sky was made, there were thick brown clouds blotted the cleansing light of the sky. I was those clouds. When the earth was made, there were rocks and mud that choked out the green of growing things. I was those rocks, and I was that mud. I was bony-eyed fish swimming through ocean depths. I was centipedes wriggling across the forest floor. I was mildew spreading tendrils across damp cave walls, filling caverns with the stench of decay.

Wherever death is, there is ugliness. And so I have been everywhere.

I recall the first time I learned that I was one thing—one despised thing —and that there was another thing outside me, one that was loved.

At that time, I was a swamp surrounding a band of travelers who had entered my depths at nightfall. They carried with them a creature in a cage, a wretched animal with torn ears and tattered fur. They had not fed it for days, and it was starving. That night, they let it out on a rope. They petted and praised it and gorged it on raw meats.

They loved me that night. They petted and fed me, too. They wore the cured skins of their conquered foes, and pierced their hands with bone needles. They stomped and shouted and distorted their faces into hideous masks.

When the creature was full and resting, watching them through satisfied half-lidded eyes, they slaughtered it. I was its entrails which they smeared across their arms and faces. I was their grunts and groans and howls; the stench of their rancid sweat; the angry slash of fire and shadow cast by their torches across their gaping mouths.

I came to love them. Ours was a strange, new synthesis. Other creatures had made themselves ugly to ward off rivals or predators, but nothing had ever before approached me with open arms and thinking minds, seeking to understand and become me. I felt myself unbound and remade as they wove me into themselves.

In the morning, they buried the dead creature. Their leader stood over its grave and intoned, "Hideous spirits that danced with us and dwelled with us, hear me. We have feasted and flattered you, and now I banish you."

With that, they left the swamp.

In the meadow beyond, they bathed themselves in the sparkling waters of the river that threaded through the grass. They rubbed their newly clean bodies with oil extracted from crushed flowers, and painted their faces with delicate shades of white and red. They sang instead of speaking, danced instead of walking. At dusk, they dined on fresh goats' milk, apples, blackberries, and honey.

I followed them as oozing mud, until there was no more mud. I circled above their heads, calling with the grating voices of birds that feast on dead things. They pretended not to hear my lonely cries. They turned away from me, seeking instead that vixen beauty whose trail I am always following, but whom I have never met.

What did she give them? Nothing but the ephemeral favor of her smile. In the end, when she left them, they returned to me. It was I, their jilted lover, who was left to tenderly trail the drool across their wizened jaws, and to twist their limbs in rigor mortis. I could have loved them all along, but they wouldn't take me until beauty fled from the rasp of their dying breaths. That day, I learned hurt. I have never forgotten it.

You, too, know hurt.

When you were born, I was born with you. Together, we felt the midwife's rough hands pull you from your mother. However, only I had enough experience of the world to recognize the fear and disgust on her face as she beheld your crippled foot.

She was quick to blink away her disdain. She wrapped us in a tight blanket and laid us on the queen's belly. "Keep them warm and comfortable," she instructed one of the ladies in waiting. "There are herbs I must fetch from my house. I will return within the hour." She was careful not to let her voice betray something had gone wrong. She had guessed that your father, the king, would blame her for your deformity.

By dusk the next day, your father's soldiers had discovered her attempting to flee the kingdom with a caravan of pilgrims headed through the mountains. Your father had her strung up on the castle gate. During your first few weeks, I hung with her, inhabiting her gnarled bones as the crows pecked them clean.

At the same time, I lay with you in your cradle as we nursed on both the queen's milk and her strained expression of sadness and distaste. She and her ladies did their best to conceal their revulsion beneath polished smiles, but even as an infant, you were not deceived. You were raised on the same provisions I'd become accustomed to over the millennia: the darting glances, cut quickly away; the whispers beneath raised hands; the unabashed stares of children too young to have learned that civil, transparent lies are considered more polite than honest acknowledgement.

Day after day, you tottered after the other children, desperate to join their games. I longed to tell you that you were not alone. I was always with you, my invisible fingers in your hair, my lips pressed against your crippled foot as a mother's lips kiss away her child's injury. Alas, you could not hear my voice, or feel my shadow.

I know your most painful secrets. Oh, yes. The ones you've consigned to memory's dusty, forsaken chambers. Their doors unlock for me. I have trespassed within them.

Don't doubt me, my prince. I could recount tales of your older brother that even you have forgotten you remember. Once, he was the center around which your thoughts revolved. Now you've learned to set him aside as a woman does with a spoiled bit of embroidery, only taking up his memory when regret inclines you to open old wounds. Your courtiers think your tense, stoic silences stem from grief, but we know the truth. Don't we?

Fear not. Your secrets are safe with me. I hated Edrian as much as you did. I loathed the beauty he wore with the entitlement of a crown prince, his shining blond hair and long flawless legs. The imperious expression he wore as he goaded the other children into racing laps through the castle's circular corridors. His grin as he watched you lurch after them, trailing behind them all, even the short, fat daughters of the duke.

Sometimes, Edrian would run beside you, breathing easy as you wheezed with the effort of dragging your useless foot. He reached out to steady you, features arrayed in a mimicry of compassion. "We'll run together," he said. He waited for you to rest your weight on his shoulders, and then he pulled away and rushed ahead, leaving you to stumble and fall as his laughter echoed through the halls, bright as birds' calls.

Again and again, he did this. Always, you thought to yourself, *this time, this time, he will help me,* and offered your trust once more.

As painful as those memories are for you, others of your memories are for me. The news of your brother's death arriving with the knights who'd ridden with him on that doomed hunt—I did not mourn his death, but I mourned what I knew it would mean for you. The sudden shower of attention bestowed on a previously unimportant son; the brocades and perfumes; the haberdashers and seamstresses and tailors.

Even I could not have predicted the southern magician, wrapped in so many layers of grey gauze that his body was blurred and indistinct, whose tales of healing miracles won him entrance into your bedchamber. He set candles smoldering in the corners of your room and knelt over them, chanting for hours, before he approached your bed. His hands emerged from his shroud, delicate and dark as carved ebony. I saw the magic on him like a shadow, and I despaired.

While you screamed with the pain of his needles and bone-breaking vises, the part of my spirit that lived within you stretched and thinned. I felt myself sifted from your flesh, like sand through a sieve.

The magician pulled aside the netting that had veiled his face. I stared into his bald, white eyes. He touched his fingers to his forehead in salute and spoke a few grave syllables to banish me. I reeled away, dizzy and spinning.

As a normal-bodied boy, you grew distant. Sometimes I watched you, inhabiting the decaying corpses of mice left on the flagstones by well-fed castle cats, or pock marks scarring the chef's daughter. I watched as you lost your thoughtful gravity. The ugly hesitate over their actions, knowing that they survive on the sufferance of the beautiful. You were comfortable, and careless, and free.

Already, you had forgotten me.

Though you don't see it, your new love betrays you as completely as your brother did. I know, for I am the foul taste that coats her tongue when she remembers your kisses, her lingering expression of disgust when she turns from your caress. You've blinded yourself to her ugliness, just as the tribe in the swamp turned deaf ears to my aching calls.

At night, as you prepare for your rest, the Lady Alna lingers outside your bedchamber to speak with your bodyguard. Through the door, you hear the murmur of her voice. You are not suspicious; it reminds you of the pleasant, reassuring hum of her sleeping breath. But I am the scar across your bodyguard's bicep where he took a blow meant for you, and I hear what she says.

She lays her hand across your bodyguard's forearm. "I've been here a year. We've hardly spoken. I don't even know your name."

Then, with a laugh: "You're so strong. Flex again. My husband must be afraid to travel without you."

"Yes, I've seen him in such moods! He does not seem to want my company either. Sometimes, he forgets I am there, and I must sit quietly and wait for his dismissal. It's kind of you to withdraw when he needs his privacy."

And leaning in, voice and lashes lowered: "The prince has confided in me that he's found the preparations for the coronation wearying. His father's death is still new and raw. He is grieving. After the ceremony, I will take him aside for a walk through the apple orchard to look at the new blossoms. Perhaps you would be so kind as to leave us alone. . . ?"

As she withdraws her hand, her fingertips brush his wrist. His muscles tense, his heart rushes, his pupils dilate. She tilts her head to the side, exposing her neck. Her wheat-colored curls are crushed against her shoulder. On the other side of the door, you wait, innocent.

Later, an abstracted look on her face, she tells you that she misses the towers of her father's city. "Go to the wizard's tower," you tell her. She smiles with the pleasure of knowing you think it's your idea, so that you will not become suspicious when she spends her afternoons there, day after day.

I am the skulls and bones and bottled screams your wizard keeps in his chamber, the premature age that gnarls his spine. I watch as the Lady Alna drops her pretense in his presence. Her shy stance becomes imperious.

She releases her hawk. He circles the room, spreading his wings with the confidence of a creature used to owning all he surveys.

Alna lays her hand on the wizard's twisted knuckles. It is her way of establishing control over men. The touch has only a dusting of magic in it, not enough to affect a man of magic. She does it anyway, for body to body has a magic of its own. Above, the hawk screams and extends his talons. He does not like it when she touches other men.

She laughs at the bird. He lands on me—one of the wizard's skulls. His talons are sharp, even against bone.

She pulls a list from her robe. "I have the Winter's Wit and Spikeleaf," she says. "I need Stitch Brew."

I extend into the wizard's crooked, toothless leer. "Stitch Brew is hard to obtain," he says.

Still, he promises to get it.

I was there the day the City of Towers burned.

The fairies of the north drove to Elithi in their icy chariots. I caught only glimpses of them as they passed, for the fairies are so beautiful that I have never seen their faces.

When they reached the city, the fairies gathered at the base of the towers. Their chancellor, who is so beautiful that I cannot see for twenty yards around him, read a statement from the fairies to the people of Elithi.

Elithi was beautiful—its spires built of finest marble, its willowy nobles dressed in whispering silks. Yet I always resided within its walls, for Elithi's beauty was purchased with ugly deeds. Some days, I watched the city from the wailing faces of maidens stolen from their homes to be sacrificed for magic spells. Others, I inhabited the severed hands and tongues cut from Elithians who'd dared speak against the city's rulers.

On the day when the fairies came to Elithi, I dwelled in the corpses of children whose organs had been harvested to make sweetmeats for the western barbarians. In the body of a disemboweled girl-child, her last breaths rattling with blood, I crawled to the tower window. The fairy chancellor's mellifluous voice echoed through the valley.

"Elithi is a blight on the ice," he said. "Its evil is a spreading blackness. For too long, we have stood aside. Our sorceresses came to us and told us of your sins. We turned them away, for the thought of destroying an entire people was too much to bear.

"Those of us who made that decision are shamed. It was only the most compassionate among us who looked not at the pain it would cause us to destroy you, but at the pain we could prevent. For years, they have traveled, filling bottles with the tears and screams and sorrows your magic has caused. Many among them have gone mad from witnessing such grief. This was their sacrifice, made in order to force us to see the agony caused by our inaction.

"To excise you from the world will hurt us. Yet it is the course of least evil. Some of us remember a world where light and dark were unalterably distinct. Now they are mixed. We stand at the estuary where they flow into each other. To stop evil, we commit evil."

As the echoes of the chancellor's voice faded, the fairies turned toward the city. In unison, they lifted their hands to the heavens. From their icy palms radiated a fiery nimbus which hung in great sheets across the air like the northern lights. Where it touched the tower walls, they burst into flame.

The Elithian nobles made a habit of living in the highest rooms, as removed as possible from the pain and despair wrought on their behalf in the city's cellars. That day, their callousness doomed them. They burned and died, their screams thrown down like falling stones.

High in the tallest tower, below only the king himself, the heir to the throne of Elithi dwelled in rooms draped in brocaded silks. His name was Honorable Karn and he lived with his young wife, the witch Alna.

They fled to the windows. Below, they heard the screams of dying peasants.

Alna stepped backward. Her wheat-colored hair was bound in braids atop her head. She pulled a dagger from the stone alter beneath the window and sawed through one of the braids. Her tongue twisted into the strange, spidery syllables of the mystic language. She had always been a wary, suspicious creature, and so she kept an arsenal of spells at her fingertips, all but complete. The beginning of this one had been cast ten years ago on a moonless midnight, over the still-beating heart cut from a priest.

Her feet rose from the ground. Her gold brocade gown trailed below her, billowing in the snap of the wind.

Her bear of a husband grabbed her skirts. She struggled. "What about me?" he growled. (I was his growl. I was his livid eyes.)

She batted him away. "Let me go, you fool."

"I won't let you desert me," said Karn. "I'll keep you here until we both burn."

Alna grimaced. I was twinned. "What do you want?"

"Make me fly."

"I can't. I only cut out one priest's heart."

"Find another way then, or we'll die together!"

Alna pursed her lips. Her pale brows drew together as she considered. "Very well," she said, "but you may not like it." She bound together another spell she'd been saving, one woven from the anguish of a bride watching her groom murdered before their consummation. Alna smiled as she began the final incantation. Karn looked up in surprise and pain as his fingers stretched out into feathers.

My prince, you must marry me. If you do not, she will kill you tomorrow. After the coronation, you will retreat with a small entourage to the castle chapel in order to receive private blessing from your priest. Alna will catch the holy man's eye. He will avert his gaze. Still, his hands will shake as he anoints your face with oil—for she has corrupted him with her whispers and wiles. He no longer has the power to call on God's protection.

The oil will dry sweet and cool on your forehead. Your wife will clasp your hand. She will lean against you, her silk gown caressing your skin. The carved gold leaves on her coronet will shine against her elaborate coiffure.

"Come walk with me," she will whisper. "I want to be alone with you."

Perhaps a tatter of memory will rustle in your mind, but you will cast aside this night's revelations as the unpleasant echoes of a nightmare.

You will take her hand. The two of you will leave the chapel. The perfume of apple blossoms will waft toward you. Your steward will release a cloud of doves that flap across your path before disappearing into the bright summer sky.

As you and Alna walk down the winding garden path, a breeze will stir the apple trees, strewing petals at your feet. Alna will step off the path, her slippered feet pale as the blossoms. She will tug your hand and pull you into the trees. Your bodyguard will follow a few steps, a nettlesome suspicion turning in his stomach, until Lady Alna turns to soothe him with her smile.

You will walk together to the orchard's heart. The sun will warm to the gold of afternoon, gilding the trunks. Veiled in the canopy's deep shadows, you will feel calm and tired. You will lie at the foot of a massive tree, resting your head on a root the thickness of your arm. Your thoughts will drift back to those days when you were an unwanted extra son, set loose to range the castle grounds alone.

Your first warning will be Karn's shadow, inscribing aerial circles with you at their center. The primordial, frightened part of your mind will recognize what it is to be prey before your reasoned self understands. You will convulse with tension, heart thumping as you struggle to your feet.

It will be too late.

Karn will descend from the sky, golden beak glinting as he dives to peck out your eyes. Behind you, Alna will begin her spell.

When your blood mixes with the packets of herbs Alna carries at her belt, a violent shuddering will overtake you. You will bleed through the skin as your soul is forced from your body. Your limbs will seize. You will choke on your tongue.

Your thoughts will rush with her betrayal. *What more could she want?*

you will wonder. You will have made her queen, the most powerful woman for kingdoms around.

It is not your kingdom she desires. She is not interested in paltry command over meadows and sheep. She craves the power of your death: the agony of a good-hearted king betrayed by his queen on the day of his coronation. In Alna's skilled hands, it will yield more power than any sorceress has possessed since the liminal years.

Karn will circle your corpse, beak bloody and glistening with the remnants of your eyes. He will caw with delight, wings spread to the wind. Alna will smile again, and hold out her wrist. He will alight there, ready to gain the first rewards of her power.

Alna will have become so powerful that she can ignite a spell with a simple gesture. She will fan her fingers, light will flare, and then Karn will be standing before her, admiring his strong hairy hands.

"Welcome back, my love," Alna will say, laughter in her voice. For she will have left him with the beady eyes and cruel beak of a hawk, commanded by a hawk's stupidly focused brain.

"I do what I please," she will tell him. "I've had enough of your jealousy."

She will fix a leather hood over his head, and a silver chain around his ankle, and she will lead him north to the frozen lands. She will kill or enslave every fairy who breathes, and then she will set them to rebuilding the elegant spires of Elithi. This time, she will be the one to sit on the throne in the highest tower. Karn will stand beside her, beak bared, a curved sword of ice grasped in his huge hairy hands, acting as both Alna's bodyguard and a warning to those who would oppose her.

Here, in the warm lands, your enemies will be emboldened. Your nation, deprived of leaders, will languish in chaos. Neighboring kingdoms will squabble over your fields. Your nobles will die on the invader's blades, your serfs marched north to be sold in Alna's Elithi.

I will dwell in more places than ever before, rolling in hideous waves across the world. Yet the heart of me will wait with you as you die, seeking to soothe your pain. Do not do that to me, my prince. Do not force me to die with you.

Accept my hand and none of this shall come to pass.

Instead, the magic will come from your professed love. Its power will allow me to take human form.

"Close your eyes," I'll say, newly incarnated. When you have, I will ease you from your bed and settle you elsewhere while I do what I must.

I will approach your queen as she sleeps in your bed, and lay my hand gently on her cheek. She will wake and behold the full, terrible strength of my ugliness. Her heart shall seize and fail. She will die with a curse on her lips.

Down in the rookery, Karn will let out a wailing cry. His talons will rip through his bonds. He will fly free, seeking to avenge his mate. As he wings to your bedroom window, I shall turn to face him. He, too, shall perish and fall.

This is the downfall of evil. They have not the courage to see the full face of ugliness, for they know it to be the appearance of their secret selves.

When they are gone, I will allow you to open your eyes. Despite how well we have known each other, you will wince, but you will not be able to draw your gaze away from me. I am riveting.

Arm in arm, we will march to the chapel. When we throw open the door, your corrupt priest will fall under the weight of his guilt. I will take his place at the altar, for ugliness has witnessed many marriages.

After we have pronounced our vows, I will take you into my arms, and we will be one again. Do not mistake me for male or female. Ugliness has no sex. Yet for you, I will be all that is feminine, that which absorbs but is yielding. I will be for you a swamp, rising around you in muddy tides that caress and engulf.

Ugliness does not deserve your rebuff. I am neither evil nor virtuous. I simply am. Since the beginning, I have been with you, yearning.

Enthroned as your queen, I will transform your lands into my flesh so that you may better rule them. Your verdant forests will lose their leaves, skeletal branches scratching against hazy skies. Dirt will choke your rivers. Your village's fair youths will stoop, their lovely maidens be afflicted with warts and lazy eyes.

The armies that lurk even now on your borders will turn back. I shall ride on their fear and transform their lands, too, into my domain. Your rule shall extend, out through all the warring kingdoms into the great empire beyond, and then further, across the vast expanse of the ocean into realms your people have never even imagined.

Someday, you will die. I will take your body into myself and sustain myself on your flesh. Your beauty will become part of me. It will ripple across our realm. What I had made hideous will be restored, but changed: even the loveliest tree with the most perfect leaves will know what it was to have been me.

I shall set your skeleton on the throne. Your skull shall rule wisely, ugly-yet-not beneath the shining gold of your crown. Fused beneath our rule, the world will know no more ugliness, no more beauty—only unity. Hate and love will spin on their axes. Flowers and weeds will be tended together; fair and blighted women sought with equal fervor. Your descendants will flourish under our wise, eternal reign.

This is the vision I offer, should you take the brave and noble risk of holding out your hand to me.

Or, refuse my offer if you must, and return to your fitful sleep beside your traitorous wife. Put aside my warnings as ghastly dreams and follow the scent of apple blossoms to your death.

Either way, I will gain your kingdom, riding in on the bloody blades of conquerors, or mounting the gilded dais on your arm. The only choice is whether I will be a slave, forced to do the will of destruction, or a wife, striving to serve my liege.

Well, my prince? Are you brave? Will you stand tall and marry me?

Or will you quiver in your bed, ridden by your cowardice until the breaking of a dim and restless dawn?

~

This story originally appeared in the anthology Subterranean: Dark Fantasy, *from Subterranean Press.*

Rachel Swirsky is a graduate of Clarion West 2005 and holds a master's degree in fiction from the Iowa Writers Workshop. Her fiction has appeared in a number of venues, including Weird Tales, Fantasy Magazine, Interzone, Subterranean Magazine, *and* Tor.com. *It's also been included in year's best anthologies edited by Jonathan Strahan, Rich Horton, and the VanderMeers.*

Dancing Lessons

Aaron Polson

The man was dead and the girl was twelve. He was stitched together and wired to a heart of brass and tin, a tiny dynamo that recharged with each step; she wore summer dresses of faded blue gingham and carried a smooth stone in her pocket. Each day for a week, she lingered after the carnival matinee and they would talk.

"You dance well for a dead man," she offered.

His grey head bobbed, but the eyes were empty buttons of dark glass. "I have little choice," he muttered.

When he was alive, the man lusted for the bottom of a whiskey bottle, and it broke him, forced him to leave his home, his wife, and his child to follow any job for food. With his world wrapped in a bindle, he rode north on a freight car. His liver gave up in tiny steps, along with his heart. The Carney found him when he was broken.

The girl came with her mother and the crowds on the first day the carnival was in town. Bright posters promised shadows of the netherworld, the end of history in fire and ice, and the dead man who, as a challenge to Lazarus, not only rose but *danced*. Her mother brought her that day, worried for her little girl's happiness. The sweet curl-headed stick of a child wore her favorite dress, thin as gauze, so lean it almost melted into her skin.

"Mother, look, a dead man who dances," she squealed.

"But dear—wouldn't you rather," her mother said, pointing at garish signs promising the wonders of the man with spider's legs, the living carousel, and a woman with an interchangeable face. She nodded at a fleshy torso stilting about on shiny copper arms. "So many other sights to see. . . ."

The girl crossed her arms and shook her head.

"Well, ride the trolley home after the show." With a weary shrug, the mother pressed a few coins in her daughter's hand and shuffled away.

The girl, filled with curiosity and cotton candy, waited until the dead man's tent emptied. She cautiously skirted the wooden benches and trampled grass, slipping through shadows at the perimeter of the tent.

"I'm dead but not blind," he said in rough tones.

———

On the second visit he explained: "It was a simple deal . . . I was dying. I was face-down in a drift of snow and the Carney pulled me to my feet. . . ."

He signed a contract before the end, a paper promise entrusting money from the carnival to his widow and his daughter. The ink dried, and his heart imploded with the whimper of a dying rabbit.

The carnival men played doctor, armed with scalpels and masks, more concerned with "could we" than "should we" they crafted an automaton of metal and flesh. Copper wires laced through the dead man's muscles along with delicate lengths of violin string. A metal stone sank into the heart-hole, and they pickled him each night in a casket of gold.

"You're dead now."

"They're taking care of my wife . . . my little girl." His weary eyes rolled in their sockets. "They own me, for now, as long as I last."

"Does it hurt, being dead?" she asked, her timid finger extending to the stitches on his arms. Her other hand played with two coins in her skirt pocket.

The dead man shook his head. "Not much."

The southern sun abused the carnival tents each afternoon.

"You look sad today," she said on their third visit.

"It's hotter here."

"Summer is coming soon." The girl smiled, but the smile faded quickly. The dead man's face moved, twisted, did a dance of its own. He looked at the girl and tried to remember—his brain was too much like a sponge in a metal dish.

"I've seen you before." His voice scratched like a twig in the dirt.

"For three days now." She grinned.

After the show, his rotting body would stiffen, sorely abused by the dancing the Carney forced him to do. He tried to shake his head, but the wires were sleeping; even the brass dynamo was nearly spent. "No, no. I've seen you before." His voice crawled on its belly. "I've seen you before, this." His hand slowly fought the mortis and tapped against his chest. "You remind me of my little girl. Your eyes, maybe."

On the fourth visit she brought him a tin cup of water she filled from a trough near the living carousel.

"For your voice," she mumbled, eyes toward the ground. The skin around his cheekbones had started to peel, fraying like loose bits of yarn.

"Thanks," he rasped.

The girl kicked at the dirt between broken strands of grass. "The smell is worse today," she said.

A nod. A sip of water loosened his throat. "It's too hot. I'm not made for the heat. But the water feels good inside."

"That's something, I suppose."

"Yes." He passed her the empty cup. "Something. Our last stop—my first with the show, was up north. Much cooler than here." His grey hand waved to the top of the tent. "The sun is unforgiving."

The girl pushed her hands into the pocket at the front of her dress and produced the smooth stone. She turned it in her hands, feeling the polished surface. "My father brought this home from France, after the war. He said it was from the Ardennes Forest. His best friend died there, and Daddy used to say a bit of him was lodged in the rock." She squinted at the stone. "I could never find that bit."

The dead man's body creaked and popped as he stood. "It's a figure of speech."

"Oh." She slipped the stone inside her pocket again. "I'll bring pictures tomorrow. Show you Daddy in his army suit."

Her mother mocked her choice of friends, but the girl dug out the cigar box under her bed and found a picture of her parents on their wedding day. Maybe the dead man could see something in the yellowed print; the dead, she heard once, have a wisdom the living cannot know.

With the stone and the photo tucked together, the girl waited until the carnival tent spilled its crowd, and she slinked inside.

"Hard day today?" she asked the slumping grey scarecrow.

He managed the slightest shoulder tic. His head rose in a slow arc, showing his face—now checkered with bone under the flesh.

"Here." She ran to this side, skipped onto the low wooden stage, and helped him to the edge. His skin hummed warmly—too warm for the dead— but she remembered the ball in his chest, the electric dynamo pushing life through his copper veins.

He didn't speak at first, but clasped at the picture she pulled from her pocket. His eyes leaked what tears they had, and the blurred man in the photo made him imagine a mirror. "I was in the war, too," he groaned. His voice faded to a whisper, not much more than a shuffle of brittle paper, as he continued. "I was in France when the trees disappeared under the rough plow of artillery shells. Ghosts rose from the mud every night and pointed at me with splinters for hands."

His eyes rolled to the top of the tent, lost and black.

The girl rested her chin on her hands. "This was my father." She pointed at the groom.

"Oh." He pushed the picture away. "He's dead?"

"I don't know." Her little fingers picked at a frayed edge of the image.

"He left us two years ago." She buried the pictured in her pocket again. "Mom said he liked whiskey better than us."

When her mother found the picture in her pocket that night, she tore it in half.

"Your father was a vagrant. A dirty, selfish vagrant."

The girl closed her eyes and set her face. Moments passed in silence.

Her mother touched her cheek with cold fingers. "What more can you expect of a dead man? He'll leave you, too. Either the carnival will move on, or. . . ."

The girl ran to the bathroom before her mother saw tears. She tore open her parent's medicine cabinet and found an old razor, untouched since his departure. The blade, although choked with rust, was still sharp, and nicked her finger. She stuffed the sore digit in her mouth and looked into the mirror, the glass darker than it should be in the early evening. She saw the dead man's face through her eyes.

On the sixth day the girl came with a bit of metal pressed in her hand. She held out the closed fingers, and transferred the blade to the dead man. "It's only a little blood," she said of a fresh scratch.

Flies danced on his rotten fingers, but buzzed away when he closed his hand around the blade. His eyes, somehow brighter now, shown between limp folds of skin. "Goodbye," he rasped as she backed from his tent.

He held the razorblade and sat on the low stage until the sounds of the carnival faded into the love song of frogs and crickets. Then, with effort, he fished for the violin strings in his legs, dug furrows in his tough flesh to find the brass cords, and severed the work of the carnival doctors. His wounds were deep and bloodless. One arm was limp—cut free too—as he brought the other arm to his chest for the brass heart, and hacked it free. The heavy orb thumped against hollow stage, rumbled across, and tumbled into the grass.

On the seventh day, his tent was empty, but the girl already knew. She waded between the tents that housed other grotesqueries for the last time, placed the torn picture of her father in uniform on his low stage, tucked it under the smooth stone from her pocket, and whispered, "Goodbye."

~

Aaron Polson *was born on the Ides of March: a good day*
for him, unlucky for Julius Caesar. He currently lives and
writes in Lawrence, Kansas with his wife, two sons, and a
tattooed rabbit. To pay the bills, Aaron attempts to teach
high school students the difference between irony and
coincidence. His stories have appeared in Necrotic Tissue,
Return of the Raven *(Horror Bound),* Monstrous *(Permuted Press), and*
other publications. You can visit him on the web at www.aaronpolson.com.

Deadglass

Lon Prater

St. Charles' Cathedral
Winespur, Appalachian Republic
September 27, 1948

The last notes of Father Holden Drury's *basso profundo* incantation faded slowly into the fleece-blanketed walls. He glanced at the inclined metal cross and the hooded man bound to it. An acute and unfounded shame made him slide his gray-flecked gaze to the floor. Weary conviction forced him to look again upon the Lord's work.

The vacant body hung there, looking smaller already; not yet dead, but diminished. Lacking a soul, the condemned's body would gradually slow and stop, winding down like a child's toy.

The leather band at his forehead wasn't tight enough to prevent the condemned from jerking violently back and forth. Up until the final verse, the poor sinner had fought against his shackles in mute frenzy, the metal clanging a dull off-tempo beat throughout the incantation.

But the bonds weren't loose enough that the condemned could come to any harm. No risk of death, or Father Drury would have had to abort the ritual. If the soul escaped before he finished the rites, it would swarm down to the Tempter, another soldier for his infernal army.

Cautiously, Father Drury picked up the thumbnail of deadglass from the holy water dish on the floor. Round eyes squinted into the enchanted glass, then widened.

He pulled a clean linen handkerchief from within his cassock; dabbed at a sun-pinkened pate now glistening with a cool mist of sweat.

Most glassbound souls were cold and filthy black, like Appalachian snow fouled by a Czech miner's boots. The one in his hand was a foggy silver-gray, and warm. It could have been crystallized motorcar exhaust.

He cocked his head, stomach lurching at the ramifications. The deadglass grew heavy in his palm.

As a priest of the Holy Cathar Church, he knew doctrine demanded containing the most dangerous souls—murderers, molesters, heretics—

preventing them from ever joining the massed hellish armies of the Infernal Twin, Thomas the Tempter. Even so, every time he performed the migration rite, a winter wind of doubt shook his faith like a birch in a blizzard.

Maybe it was the wet tongue of the Tempter slithering around in his mind. Or perhaps it was the anonymity of a tongueless head under the tamper-sealed canvas hood. Whatever the cause, until he held the loveless cold crystal in his hand, saw its sin-blackened impiety with his own two eyes, he always nursed a seed of doubt as to whether migration was justified.

This time, for once, he had been right to doubt.

The innocent glass trembled in his hand. Absently, he slipped it into a pocket of the black suit jacket he wore beneath his cassock.

Guilt gnawed at the muscles of his jaws, both for migrating an innocent and for the sin he was about to commit. He approached the empty body butterfly-pinned to the metal cross. The condemned wore only the canvas hood and a coarse paper gown.

As Father Drury watched, the man's chest swelled slightly, drawing another shallow automatic breath. The space between each breath grew longer and longer.

The priest kneeled, not to say the benediction, not yet, but to search the body for identifying marks. He looked over his shoulder at the door to the windowless, soundproofed room, certain he would be caught in his sin at any moment.

The condemned man would have been as tall as Father Drury, but leaner. Where the priest resembled a rosy-skinned lumberjack, burly and barrel-chested, the body before him was lanky and tanned. A garden of curly black hairs overran its chest and forearms.

The priest checked his heavy wristwatch. Ticking faster than usual, the rotter! He bit back a curse and tugged the hood's neckband up, careful not to break the tamper seal.

With the sealed bottom pulled snug against the man's jawbone, the priest noted a pair of moles over the Adam's apple. He ran a finger across fine stubble like spilt black pepper. It matched the rest of the body hair, so it was a safe bet the man sported black hair on his head as well.

Father Drury shrugged off the insistent voice of his training, blanked out the awareness that he was betraying every tenet of the Phased Migration doctrine. He slid the neckband down into place.

He tried to feel the man's face through the stiff canvas with no success. His groping fingers met only the suggestion of a large bent nose, and perhaps a full, luxuriously thick head of hair beneath the hood. Impossible to be sure through the fabric.

This was taking too long, and he had not yet said the benediction. Were those steps he heard? Surely not. The walls were soundproofed, weren't they? He checked the body again.

Its breathing was nearly undetectable. The soulless heart beat with less force now; color drained from the upturned, shackled hands.

But not all color, he noticed. The sisters of St. Joan's order were supposed to cleanse and sanitize the condemned before migration. They hadn't been able to remove all of the black powder ground-in around his nails.

A coal miner? No, the skin was too weathered, those limp hands too soft. Someone so tall would have spent miserable days stooped over in the mines.

The doorknob rattled. Father Drury assumed a position of prayer as the padded door cracked open. Silence reigned for a long moment as he murmured the final words of the benediction. Then Sister Matilda's voice: "Father, may we enter?"

"Certainly, Sister, I was just finishing up." His voice sounded more strained than he liked.

"Is all well?" she asked as she stepped into the migration chamber, two junior nuns in tow. "Sister Carla could get you some iced tea."

He stood up, brushing at his knees. "No thank you, that won't be necessary. I just need some fresh air."

Her pursed lips reminded him of two prunes pressed together. "You know what's best," she said, gracing him with a superficial smile.

Sister Matilda was all business. She and the Agnite sisters would not begin preparing the body for the disposal rites until he left the room.

Father Drury bid the sisters good day. He closed the fleece-lined door behind him, leaving the nuns to their work.

The bishop was a jowly man, rounded and soft from years of study and administration. The only things hard about him were his river-pebble eyes. He gestured with a pudgy hand for Father Drury to sit in a wing chair by the window that overlooked the Bishopric of Richmond. "Good to see you, again. Holden, is it? To what do I owe the pleasure?"

"This," Father Drury said, leaning forward in his seat. He set the deadglass on the bishop's polished desk. It clicked.

The bishop's pebble eyes flickered. He drew in a sharp breath. "Why haven't you given this to the Souls Custodian?"

"Isn't it obvious?" Father Drury pointed at the deadglass. "There's been a mistake. This soul is innocent!"

The bishop's voice became as hard as his glance. "Impossible. Every phase of the migration process, condemnation to disposal and storage, is governed by doctrine. Procedures and rituals over a thousand years old." He stabbed one fat finger at Father Drury. "How dare you, of all people, a priest —a *Migrator*, no less—question the very process that holds the Twin at bay!"

The bishop's ferocity took Father Drury aback. He sat up a little straighter in his chair, putting a steadying hand on the padded armrest.

"Your Reverence," he began cautiously. "I have condemned twenty-three sin-blackened souls to the glass. Compared to those others, this one is ready for sainthood. Surely there is some explanation?"

This time the bishop fought visibly to control his emotions. He fussed with a shirt button, then with a pen that lay on the desk. He chewed his bottom lip, glaring at Father Drury all the while.

When he finally spoke, the bishop chipped off every word like cold, hard cemetery granite. "Are you one of the three cardinals on the Condemnation Board?"

He continued without waiting for a response. "Are you privy to the inner sanctum of the Pontiff? No? Then I suggest to you, Father, that the questions you ask are improper. *At best.* I further suggest that you let this matter go, before you find yourself ministering to a cold and remote parish."

Father Drury bowed his head, keeping the anger and astonishment from his face. The bishop's response seemed out of proportion. He stood up, wiping rigid hands on his thighs reluctantly, as if he'd found something greasy on them and could find no other cloth.

"I understand, Your Reverence," he said formally. "I'll deliver this soul to the Depository immediately."

The bishop's icy demeanor seemed to thaw. He flashed a cool smile, one that said he was glad to have all the, *ahem*, unpleasantness behind them. But that smile didn't quite reach his eyes.

"That won't be necessary, Holden," the bishop said. "I'll make sure it gets over to Brother LaFayette." The bishop lumbered to his feet.

Father Drury took a backward step. "If there's nothing else, Your Reverence?"

"No, no. I don't want to keep you any longer." The bishop picked up the shiny deadglass and looked at it thoughtfully.

Father Drury turned and marched to the door. As he grasped the ornate brass handle, the bishop spoke.

"Holden?"

Father Drury pivoted. The late afternoon sun streamed in through a frost-lined window, silhouetting the bishop's squat wide frame. "Yes, Reverence?"

"Sin is measured not by its effects on Man and Earth, but by the degree to which it benefits the Twin. You know that, don't you?" the bishop asked without turning around.

It was simple truth, one that summarized nearly a millennia of post-Trentian Cathar thought.

"Yes, Reverence. Of course."

The bishop held the deadglass up between a thumb and fingertip. The little disc sparkled as if with its own light, scattering multicolored bits of cold sun dancing around the room. "Even the smallest, best-intended sin could hasten the Twin's return, remember that."

"And what of my own soul, Reverence? Is robbing an innocent man of God's Love such a petty sin to worry over, then?"

The bishop closed his fist upon the deadglass even as Father Drury crossed the threshold.

When he wasn't engaged as a Migrator, Father Drury spent his days working on a history of the Crusades against the Greco-Pauline mystery cults and filling in when needed at St. Filbert's Cathedral on High Street. St. Filbert's boasted the fourth largest library in Richmond; in fact, it was among the largest in the Appalachian Republic.

This morning it seemed smaller than he remembered, more closed up. The bookshelves leaned in upon him, and the air smelled warm and stale like two-week-old bread. He forced himself to finish reading a gloomy, uninspired analysis of Seigfried IV's failed assault on Athens, then slammed the thick tome shut. He needed a change of scenery.

He tumbled out into the busy river of Richmond's sidewalks, headed east. He was grateful for the crisp wind and open sky, and did his best to ignore the noise of the finned and chromed automobiles lurching through the streets.

He told himself he was going to the city's library, the one by the Jefferson Grozny Memorial, to fetch an obscure reference and perhaps have lunch at the Croatian diner on the corner. If anyone would have asked, that's what he would have told them as well; but it wasn't altogether true.

He planned to look through the sheaves of dailies in the smaller library's basement, to see who had gone missing recently. He didn't have any business doing so; the bishop had ordered him to forget the whole incident. Nonetheless, he felt called to learn what he could of the relatively sinless soul he had migrated, and he followed.

"Fell behind on the Patrick and Trotsky strip, Stephen," he said to the smiling, birdlike librarian. The lie rolled out too easily for Holden's comfort. He felt queasy.

Holden bit the insides of his fleshy cheeks, then continued: "It's my one guilty pleasure, you know. I'd like to get caught up with those rascals, if you keep the papers handy."

Stephen smiled at him and winked like a conspirator. "Your secret is safe with me, Father." Holden hated himself for the untruth, but quibbled no more as Stephen ushered him into an unventilated basement room full of newspapers and cobwebs.

Holden put his hand on the room's only piece of furniture: a rickety table that cringed beneath a bright, bare bulb hanging from the ceiling. This hot little room was hardly better than St. Filbert's news archive. The difference was that here he could look for what he wanted in private.

One hour melted into another. The Holy Cathar Church simply abducted those whose souls the Board condemned, leaving the families and police to wonder at the sinner's sudden disappearance. Most ended up here, in the local headlines, obituaries, and police reports. Holden scanned the papers mechanically, trying his best to ignore the heat and his empty, protesting stomach.

Touching the newsprint left his thick fingers smudged with ink. The handkerchief, formerly white, grew blacker every minute. He swabbed sweat from his broad forehead, trying not to get any ink on himself. It was a lost cause from the start.

At five o'clock, he surrendered to the heat and his howling stomach. He trudged up the dusty wooden stairs to the library. Two months of dailies, and he had found nothing relevant.

"Your sin is showing, Father. Everyone will know what you've been up to," Stephen said from behind the desk.

Holden's heart skipped. He moved his lips without speaking, his mind calculating the best response.

Stephen wrinkled his hawk nose at him. "You have the ink from those Patrick and Trotsky strips all over your face and hands. You can wash up in the staff water closet if you'd like."

Father Drury grunted, glad he hadn't spoken. Maybe this was a sign from the Lord, a warning that he should mind the Bishop's counsel and forget the deadglass. Or it could be old Thomas the Tempter, tweaking a priest's nose for simple sport.

"Right through that door, Father, left of the biographies." The big priest thanked him and strode off in that direction.

In the restroom, Holden took a scratchy washcloth from the stack and wet it in the sink. He scrubbed his round face until it shone pinker than usual, then set to work on his hands. The ink came off easily for the most part, except for the crevices around his fingernails.

The realization exploded like a stick of dynamite just behind his breastbone. There had been an article about a man who had escaped from jail, a typesetter accused of using his employer's presses to print "unsavory" pamphlets on the night shift. The police remained mystified as to how he had escaped. As far as they knew, he was still on the loose.

"You fool!" Holden said to the mirror. A typesetter. Just the sort of man to have stubborn black stains around his fingers. He should have made the connection on the spot, but he had been looking for disappearances, not fugitives.

Father Drury flung the washcloth onto the sink and shot from the restroom like all the Tempter's armies chased behind him. Stephen made a surprised noise as Father Drury barreled back down into the basement room, but did not follow.

The frenzied priest pulled two boxes away from the wall and tore into a third. A quarter of the way down, he found what he was looking for. He jerked upright with a high-pitched yelp that didn't fit his big frame.

Wayne Charnick. He read the article three times, his eyes bouncing excitedly like the words were insects darting across the page. Wayne Charnick had worked as a night typesetter at a small press downtown for over three years. A few weeks ago, his employer caught him printing "foulness" and had him jailed. He had disappeared from the jail cell the next night, presumed to be armed and dangerous. A reward had been offered for any information on his whereabouts.

There wasn't a picture with the article, but it did list a sister, Mina Charnick, who lived in Doveburton, just a few winding mountain miles from out-of-the-way Winespur, and the facilities at St. Charles'. Holden looked down at his gently quivering hands. Not only were they once again marked with ink, but now they were also damp. He couldn't be sure whether the moisture came from having just washed them or from the clamminess of cold sweat.

He heaved the boxes of archived newspapers back into place. The man had been printing some kind of foulness, yet his glass had contained so little sin. Pornography rarely led to migration, but there was another kind of printed work that would surely draw the church's ire: *heresy.*

But what heresy would leave a glass all but untainted?

Father Drury stared at the knot of his ink-smudged hands. He was reminded of Duke Tartan's mother, from the old Scottish play. She'd eventually had her consort cut off both of her hands, unable to bear the sight of her son's blood upon them.

He muttered a soft, grumbling prayer and turned to the basement stairs. As he ascended to the library, each of the ancient wooden steps groaned in turn, as if the big priest and his guilt weighed too much for them to bear.

Unpaved mountain roads made the long, slow ride to Doveburton painful and difficult. The old twelve-seater bus bumped about on the road like an impure woman on a rented mattress. Father Drury chided himself for the image. The jarring ride left him with a sore neck.

Small penance, considering what he probably deserved.

He stepped off the bus and looked around. The Doveburton bus stop was a crowded, dingy affair. He twisted his head around each way, working the soreness out with a few satisfying clicks and pops. Holden got directions from an attendant before setting off to Mina Charnick's house at a respectable pace.

When he got there, a lean woman with a hard, lined face sat smoking on the front porch steps. She glared at his collar and cassock, saying nothing.

"Miss Charnick?"

"I don't know where he is, Father."

"Well that makes two of us," Holden said, conscious of the half-lie.

Awkward silence filled the space between them. "I figured all you church folk and police woulda give up on finding him by now."

"Beg pardon?" Holden asked, a little more alert.

"When he first got ketched, all you church folk come out here asking about the papers he was making, but he never brought none of it around here, so I never saw it. Then the police come, looking for anything they could use agin' him, and they couldn't find nothing neither, so they quit coming round here."

She puffed on the cigarette. "Till he got out that cell. Then the police all come a runnin' back. I wondered why it'd take the church so long to check back. But you're wasting your time, Father. I still ain't seen my brother Wayne. Not since before he got ketched."

Holden raised his eyebrows. "Mind if I sit?" He flashed a congenial grin and hunched down beside her before she could object. "Do you have a picture of him?" he asked, his voice so soft it barely carried in the thin air.

She cocked her head, looking at him crookedly. "I might."

"My name is Father Holden Drury," he ventured. It was late for introductions, but he wasn't sure what else to say. How do you tell a woman you may have migrated her brother's innocent soul into a piece of glass? "I'm trying to find him. He may have been—may be innocent, but I have to find him to prove it."

The woman snorted smoke all over Father Drury. "And a pitcher will help you do that? Don't you people even know what Wayne looks like?"

He didn't like leading Mina Charnick on. There was no way he could help her brother; the glass was a perfect inescapable cell, and by now his body had been immolated. Holden had sinned several times already today, lying to find some truth. To discover whether the migration of Wayne Charnick had been justified. By the end of the day he would likely have much more to repent.

"I wish I did, Miss Charnick. It would make it easier to help him."

Another long moment passed. The woman popped to her feet. She stubbed the cigarette out against the flaking paint of the porch rail and flicked the butt out into the yard.

"You wait here," she said, staring at him through rheumy, narrowed eyes.

A few minutes later she returned, pushing the door open just enough to shove a cheap metal picture frame into his chest.

"It was in a fire," she said, lower lip on the verge of trembling. "Take it, and don't none of you come back here till Wayne's home safe."

Holden took the frame. It had indeed been in a fire at some point, but must have been saved or salvaged early enough to prevent all but a slight warping of the glass. Holden's gaze went straight to the throat of the happy man in the picture, to the twin moles resting there.

Holden thought of the old Carib stories of natives who wouldn't let their pictures be taken, for fear the camera would also take their souls. He resisted the urge to wince, and likewise the urge to reach out and comfort the pitiable woman on the other side of the door. The only hope he could give was false, and probably unwelcome to boot.

Holden nodded a somber 'Good day' before trudging back to the bus station. He clutched the frame in one hand as he walked. Every so often he would steal a look at the photo and see more than he wanted to in the lopsided grin, a whimsical knowledge hidden in those laughing eyes. When he could look no more, he put the scratched metal frame and the heretic it contained away.

Not all souls went to Heaven, or even to the Tempter's Hell. Some ended up here, in this shabby brown building some dying sinner had traded to the church for a window seat on the ride to Eternal Bliss. Father Drury had spent the last six days praying and fasting. He had considered going again to the bishop, but dropped the idea as soon as he had it. The fat little man would make good his threat with happy zeal. *Sin is measured not by its effects on Man and Earth, but by the degree to which it benefits the Twin.*

But which sin served old Thomas the Tempter more? Migrating an innocent soul or leaving a heretic free to print what he would? How could the Condemnation Board be certain they had chosen the right course?

Holden bit off the thought as he crossed the threshold of the Church's Depository. Here in this building the monks of St. Brion's Order served as custodians: not only of deadglass, but also of heretical writings, apocrypha, Greco-Pauline idols, and other relics deemed too impure for hallowed ground. The Brionites also had the unenviable task of collecting the sinners who had been condemned to migration.

Father Drury adjusted his chafing collar and looked about him. The foyer was reasonably well appointed, evidence of the Brionite's current favor with the Pontiff. Some of the lesser orders, like the Knights of Cortez, were rarely funded well enough to heat their facilities all winter long.

The click of Holden's steps on the marble floor made the monk at the entry desk start. The worried little man slid something beneath his logbook and beamed up at Holden.

"You surprised me, Brother Drury. Have you brought us another lost soul? Who is it this time . . . Churchill?"

Holden smiled, scanning a board filled with names and titles. "You know I could not tell you, Brother Sergei, even if I knew. But I am here on Migration business." He paused, then: "Is LaFayette in?"

The young clerk growled. "That old goat is always in." A buzzer sounded. "You know the way." The big priest started toward the iron-banded door then doubled back. He snatched at the logbook, revealing a page of newsprint. Cartoon strips.

"Your duties, Brother?" he asked gravely.

Sergei looked sheepish. "I'll throw them away."

Holden hesitated, then folded it and put it into a pocket. "No, Brother, I think I'll hold on to them." He smiled at the monk like they shared a secret. "And if it's today's edition, I'll refrain from reporting this incident to the Custodian of Heretical Writings." He winked.

Brother Sergei returned a relieved smile. "Oh, it is. Besides, Brother Gustav is with the Bishop today, so you'd have to wait to turn them over. You will dispose of it for me?"

"That suits me perfectly." Holden winked at Brother Sergei, who again pressed the access buzzer.

Holden pushed the thick door open and strode through it, smiling. He wouldn't be seeing LaFayette, or at least he hoped not. And with the Custodian of Heretical Writings away, it would be easier than he thought to get his hands on a copy of whatever Wayne Charnick had been printing.

Or so he thought. The great metal door marked 'False Writings' was encumbered with an old padlock as big as Holden's fist. Closer examination revealed the hasp wasn't really so thick. A well-placed blow (maybe two) from the fire axe mounted next to the roll of red hose on the wall would have him inside. But it would also draw unwanted attention. He needed a place to hide, somewhere he could wait until after hours.

The broom closet at the end of the hall would work. As he walked in that direction, a small part of Holden's mind noted how easy it was becoming for him to think and do sinful—even criminal—things. Breaking and entering to read heresy hardly drew a protest from his inner voice at this point. And misrepresentation—lying—was becoming second nature. Some part of him asked: *Holden, old boy, is clearing your own guilty conscience worth all of this sin?* But the stiller, smaller voice within knew this was no sin at all.

Holden jerked awake, aching and blind. For a long moment his heart raced. The air hung unmoving and stale, thick with dust and a sterile smell.

He wondered if this was what it was like to be trapped in the deadglass.

No, he could still hear the deep-toned bells from St. Francis De Molay's cathedral two blocks over. He was in a broom closet, a cramped one, at ten o'clock at night. The bells had startled him awake, but he'd been too groggy to count them when they first began ringing. Regardless, the building would be empty at this hour. Empty enough to get into the False Writings Depository, at any rate.

He reached around in the dark until one hand found the light switch. He stopped himself. The light would only ruin his night vision. Groping quietly in the cramped little room, Holden felt the cool metal of the doorknob. He gave the knob a little twist, opened the door a careful inch, and listened.

Absolute quiet. *Perfect.*

The big priest—would he still be able to call himself a priest in the morning?—stepped lightly into the hall, shutting the door behind him. Small windows pierced the top of the wall every ten feet or so. Just enough light seeped through to allow him to move around. So long as he didn't go too fast, he wouldn't bump into anything he didn't want to.

Holden loosened his collar. The skin beneath it felt raw, as if enraged at such a man as he for daring to wear a priest's collar. Holden rubbed the sore flesh with the tips of two fingers. There was no soothing it, so he left the collar loose as he crept toward the fire station he had scouted out earlier.

A few minutes later, Holden stood outside the False Writings Depository, finding the hasp with his fingers. One whack with the fire axe, a few breathless minutes straining his ears against the silence, a two-handed push on the heavy door, and he was in.

Once the door had shut, he turned on the lights. No sense worrying about night vision now, he mused. He wouldn't be able to find what he needed in the dark, much less read it. After his eyes adjusted to the sudden glare, he looked around. Shelves full of boxes, each numbered and labeled, stood in strict formation like soldiers.

Getting in proved to be the easy part. When Holden found the index, it was encoded. He bit back a curse.

Not sure what else to do, he checked a few containers at random. He found plenty that would have interested him another time, including a translation of some of Paul's letters, but nothing relevant to Wayne Charnick's heresy.

After more than an hour, he dropped to the floor, despairing. *Am I here for a reason, Lord? Am I meant to find something?* He pulled out Wayne Charnick's picture, stared at that unchanging face smiling from behind the fire-warped glass. Holden sat there in silent meditation a few moments more before he got back to his feet.

He put the picture down on a bare spot of the Custodian of False

Writing's desk and half-heartedly searched through the drawers and in-basket for any clue as to the index's code, or the location of Wayne Charnick's papers.

Finding nothing, he looked again at the heretic's picture grinning at him from the desk. The glass had flowed as it melted, making it a little thinner on one side. Charnick still held that unaccountably happy frozen stare, as if unaware his picture had been through the flames and back—

Holden snatched up the picture and broke into a run, thinking crazily: *That's it! It doesn't matter either way!* He didn't bother to turn out the lights as he burst from False Writings and into the darkened hallway; but he did make sure to pick up the axe.

When he broke in to the Souls Depository, Holden was certain that he was no longer qualified to be called a priest. The tender flesh around his neck had stopped aching for just a few precious moments as he ran to the room where the glass-bound souls were stored. The coolness of the air as he moved his big body through it refreshed him.

Made him forget about guilt and innocence and the doctrines of sin, if only for a moment.

When he couldn't find the one soul he wanted out of the thousands being stored here, it enraged him. *How dare the Church make it so hard to save one innocent soul?*

It no longer mattered to him what Charnick had been printing; he hardly cared at all about that now. What mattered to Holden was that he had migrated an innocent soul, and that act had stained his own soul as surely as the hair had abandoned the top of his pink head.

The warped glass in the picture frame had made him think of it. *It was in a fire,* Mina Charnick had said. Fire indeed. One hot enough to melt glass might be hot enough to burn free the innocent soul trapped within.

Setting the blaze had been easy enough. The church was over-confident. The bishop was over-confident. None of them even considered the possibility that their doctrines and procedures could be fallible, much less breached.

Perhaps sin had everything to do with man and earth; maybe the truly guilty were those who ignored that fact.

Holden stayed inside the Souls Depository until the heat blazed so intensely from the scorching walls that it took his breath. He half-imagined he could hear every last one of the glassbound souls cracking free of their crystal prisons and going on to wherever they were meant to. He pushed the front door open and sprinted down the hall, not knowing whether to laugh or sob at what he had wrought.

While he ran, Holden fumbled at the collar and tightened it back into place, despite the rawness beneath. Warm ashes kissed his cheeks. His skin and clothes were already black with soot. It didn't matter; he laughed and charged through the quiet halls all the faster for it.

He'd almost regained control of himself when he barreled past the vacant entry desk and through the front doors, bursting out into the cool, cloudless night. He sat down on the curb across from the Depository and watched the eastern wing burn.

Outside in the October air, his head seemed somehow clearer, as if he had been howling drunk and became suddenly sober. The giddy sense of freedom from guilt had risen then dissipated like the column of smoke looming above the burning brown building.

The church would send someone to collect him; it was certain. He would have to pay for all of the guilty souls he had released. He wondered about the penance they would impose on him; most likely his own soul would be condemned to the glass, the first of a new sin-menagerie.

The muscles around his mouth twisted into a wry, sad smile. Migration did more than the Holy Cathar Church realized; more than just keeping a soul from serving in the Tempter's Army. Binding a soul in glass also guaranteed that it would never know sin—or feel guilt—again.

The glass offered a peculiar species of freedom.

Sirens approached. They would be too late to save the building. Too late to save any souls tonight, his own included.

The wind no longer blew cool, having taken on the heat of the rising flames. Holden adjusted his collar with sooty, sweating fingers, ignoring the soreness beneath. The black circles around his fingernails reminded him of Wayne Charnick. Would his own bit of glass prove as cool and pale? Had he done enough to cleanse it?

He shoved his hands through the cassock, looking for Charnick's picture but finding the Patrick and Trotsky strip but instead. He must have set the heretic's picture down when he'd picked up the ax. The glass in that frame would melt for sure this time, the picture would curl up, blacken and rise into the heavens on a pillar of heat.

Holden's face tightened as waited there in air so warm it dried his tears. Just as the fire fighters had the flames under control, a man wearing a ceremonial hairshirt and circle-wrapped olivewood cross approached.

"Father Drury, you have been condemned," the Brionite said by way of introduction. "Come with me."

If they had sent Brother Sergei, Holden would have returned the folded-up comic page to him. Maybe even clapped the monk on the back, thanking him for one last laugh. But this wasn't Sergei, and he wouldn't understand.

Holden wiped his hands on his trouser legs. "Right behind you, brother," he said, looking up into the smoke filled sky. "Lead me not into temptation."

~

A version of this story originally appeared in Writers of the Future XXI.

Lon Prater *is an active duty Naval officer by day, writer of odd little tales by night. His short fiction has appeared in the Stoker-winning anthology* Borderlands 5, Writers of the Future XXI, *and Origins Award finalist* Frontier Cthulhu. *Check out www.LonPrater.com to find out more.*

Perchance to Dream

D.J. Cockburn

Pongo Ponsonby thought he was dead, but he wasn't sure. He decided to ask his flight leader. "Blue three to blue leader, blue three to blue leader. . . ."

The flat sound of his voice stopped him. What was he going to say next? He'd have to buy drinks for every officer in the mess if he asked if he was dead. Besides, he couldn't feel the transmit button under his finger, so no one would hear him. Now that he thought about it, he couldn't feel anything in his hands. Just something under his back. And someone patting his chest. Someone who breathed heavily.

He groaned. The last thing he remembered was cannon shells from a Messerschmitt he hadn't even seen, tearing his Spitfire apart around him. He must have bailed out somehow but he'd been over France when he was shot down, so whoever was patting him was probably a German taking him prisoner. Damn.

The hands fumbled along his belt. He opened his eyes to a sky heavy with mist, and saw that he was lying on the bank of a still, dark river. This wasn't a hospital, and the hands belonged to a wizened old man whose loincloth didn't look like it was issued by a Wehrmacht quartermaster.

The old man gave a satisfied grunt and undid Pongo's belt buckle. Pongo remembered the gold coins sewn into it, standard issue for operations over occupied territory.

He sat up sharply. "Hey! Stop that! *Arrètez-vous!*"

The old man scuttled backward.

"You—you old!" Pongo stifled the word that sprang to his lips. He'd never be able to look the vicar in the eye if he swore at an old man.

A deep growl in his right ear filled Pongo's nostrils with the smell of recently eaten meat. Pongo's shoulders tensed. He'd never been fond of dogs, and that didn't sound like a small one.

He turned to look at the source of the growl. He found himself looking into the jaws of a dog the size of a carthorse with a set of teeth that would make a tiger envious, but what made Pongo leap to his feet were the two other identical heads attached to the same body.

Pongo looked around to see if the old man had any idea how to cope with the monster, but he was paying no attention to the dog. He was haranguing Pongo in a language that sounded vaguely familiar, but wasn't French or German.

The man said something that sounded less guttural, and Pongo thought he caught a word, '*aurum*'. Then another one: '*doné*'. A memory of Pongo's schooldays surfaced, in which he was bent over Old Cribb's desk with his trousers around his ankles, answering Old Cribb's questions in that same language and making sure he got it right because the cane wasn't slow to point out any mistakes. The language was Latin, and the more guttural language had been ancient Greek. So he wasn't in France. He was dead after all, and Cerberus the hellhound was going to have some more meat to foul his breath if Pongo didn't pay the ferryman.

He found his pocket knife, cut through the seam of his belt, and handed the old man a coin. The dog stopped growling, but the string of saliva that fell from the middle mouth didn't look friendly.

The old man was frowning at the coin. "This coin is not Greek or Roman," he said, still in Latin.

Pongo blessed Old Cribb, cane and all, when he understood. "It's a coin of Britannia."

"Then the price is two coins."

Pongo recalled the song that advised, 'you can't take your dough when you go go go,' and reflected that the lyricist would have to think again when he discovered that not only money but also inflation had preceded him. A look at Cerberus convinced him to hand over another coin.

The old man pointed across a field covered by a web of mist. "Go there for judgment, and if they send you back, tell whoever buries you to put the coin in your mouth next time. It makes my job much easier."

He waddled away, giving Cerberus an absent-minded pat in passing. Cerberus lay down and closed all six eyes.

Pongo found himself alone by the river, wondering why he'd spent every Sunday morning of his nineteen years being told what to do to get to a heaven that didn't extend invitations to three-headed dogs or septuagenarian extortionists. He wanted to sit down and wrap his arms around his knees until someone came to tell him that it was all right. He'd done that when he was twelve and had been winded on the rugby field. The only person who came was the divinity master, who dragged him to his feet and told him that Waterloo wasn't won by crying. Not even the divinity master would come for him here.

At least it had been quick. Not like Harry, whose Spitfire had burned all the way down from ten thousand feet.

Poor Harry had been the only constant in Pongo's life since they met amid the genteel brutality of boarding school. They had somehow managed to stay together until they ended up in the same squadron. Then they'd both been killed in action, which meant that Harry would be here.

The thought focused Pongo's eyes in the direction the old man had pointed. He could just make out a pool through the mist, with three figures beside it. If that was where he'd been sent, it was probably where Harry had been sent. Pongo strode toward the pool, through the knee-high asphodels that splashed him with dew.

The three figures were all young men, dressed in splendid purple robes. They were all staring at him in open-mouthed amazement.

"*Salveté,* patricians," said Pongo as cheerfully as he could.

For a moment, none of them moved, then the one in the middle replied. "Oh, er, yes, *salvé.*"

The man on the left kicked the speaker's shin and glared at him. All three made a visible effort to throw back their shoulders and arrange their features into expressions of grim dignity. They reminded Pongo of the school chaplain when he and Harry had chanced upon him urinating behind a hedge.

The one in the middle spoke again, employing the same grave tone that the chaplain had used on that unfortunate day. "Welcome, shade, to the Pool of Memory, where we shall judge your conduct in the Middle World and decide your fate in the Underworld."

Pongo found the idea of being judged something of a relief. It was something he'd expected. He moistened his lips and startled himself by saying "Jolly good" in English.

The speaker frowned. "I am King Aeacus. This is King Rhadamanthys and King Minos. We shall decide your doom."

He glared at Pongo, who put his hands behind his back and stared straight ahead. Headmasters and wing commanders appreciated that pose, so perhaps judges of the dead did too. The deepening furrows on Aeacus's brow suggested otherwise.

"His name," hissed Rhadamanthys.

Aeacus looked relieved. "Speak your name, shade."

Pongo felt like a new recruit, and he knew how recruits were supposed to behave. He snapped to attention. "Ponsonby! WR! Pilot Officer! Five-oh-nine-two-one-oh! *Sir!*"

That sounded rather formal so he added, "Most people call me Pongo."

The three judges exchanged glances. Pongo wondered if he'd said something wrong, but he could hardly be blamed for his name, could he?

Aeacus was glaring again.

"His land," hissed Rhadamanthys.

Aeacus nodded. "What land do you owe your fealty, shade?"

"Britannia."

Aeacus started. Rhadamanthys and Minos looked as though their eyes were about to leap from their heads, but managed to retain their dignified poses.

"There are those in Britannia who follow the Olympians?" asked Minos. "After all these centuries?"

"I'm sorry?" said Pongo.

"Perhaps we should explain our confusion," said Minos. "No shades have arrived here for more than a thousand years. Now you arrive, dressed. . . ." he waved a hand at Pongo's Irvine jacket and Mae West life jacket. They made a shabby contrast to the judges' regalia.

"Your name makes no sense in any civilized language," said Minos. "You say you're from an island that has hardly sent us anyone since the Romans left. What are you doing here?"

Pongo's shoulders sagged. They wouldn't be so surprised if Harry had come this way. "I'm sorry. I don't know why I'm here either."

Rhadamanthys sniffed. "Of course he doesn't know. Why bother asking a mortal?"

"It might be important," said Minos. "If there's been a resurgence of the old religion, we'll need more space down here and I'd bet my minotaur that they'll forget to tell us."

"Of course they will," said Aeacus. "Remember when Alexander started converting the Persians? No one warned us, and they were queuing up to their waists in the Styx while we looked for somewhere to put them."

"Then we'd better ask the appropriate authorities," Rhadamanthys glanced upward. "The shade knows nothing."

Pongo was used to feeling overlooked, but he had hoped that whoever was supposed to be judging his immortal soul would at least remember he was there. "Excuse me, but I'm Christian. Church of England."

The glare of the judges reminded him that recruits didn't speak until they were spoken to.

"Let us get the judgment out of the way, then we can discuss the important matters," said Rhadamanthys.

Minos and Aeacus nodded, and all three resumed their stern expressions.

"What was your profession, shade?" asked Aeacus.

That was a difficult question. Pongo didn't know the Latin for 'Spitfire pilot', and Icarus probably hadn't set a very good precedent. "I'm a warrior."

Aeacus snorted. "A warrior indeed! Then why are you wearing fancy dress? A young warrior like you should die in battle, not at a masque."

"I did die in battle. This is my uniform."

"Then where is your weapon? Why were you not clutching it at the end? Did you throw it down and run?"

A weapon that weighed two tons and carried you along at three-hundred-and-fifty knots would be outside Aeacus's experience. "My weapon was destroyed."

"Very well. Have you seen much battle in your short life?"

Pongo hadn't seen much else since he and Harry got off the train at Biggin Hill, two lifetimes ago. "Six months of constant fighting."

"How many enemies have you bested?"

Pongo swallowed. He'd known they'd have to get round to that, and lying wouldn't help. His voice faltered as he admitted his only cardinal sin. "Four confirmed kills, two probables."

He was about to beg their forgiveness, but all three were nodding with what looked like approval.

"Four dead enemies is a good epitaph for such a young man," said Minos. "Very good indeed."

"That alone qualifies him for Elysium," said Rhadamanthys. "Whatever else he may have done."

"I don't think we need to know anything else," said Aeacus, "and we need to find out if we're going to get a sudden rush. Go through that, young man. They'll find you some proper clothes when you get there."

Pongo looked around to see something that looked like a rectangular hole in whatever reality he had fallen into. It seemed to be standing on the ground but as Pongo got closer, he saw that it was not a hole but something dark that looked as solid as glass but neither revealed anything on the other side nor reflected Pongo as he approached it. He squinted at it until it filled his vision. He felt a lurch like looping the loop after six pints.

Sunlight burst on his face and the chords of a lyre caressed his ear. He shaded his eyes against the light, and he found himself in a field of deep green grass. He was surrounded by bearded men in leather armor, lying against cypress trees or dancing to the lyre music.

Then he saw the girl playing the lyre, and forgot everything else. It wasn't just that she had the sort of lissome beauty that he associated with the novels of Sir Walter Scott, but that her gown was cut below her breasts. Pongo had never seen real breasts before, although he'd stared at plenty of blouses and tried to divine the shapes concealed beneath. Harry once said that he'd seen Madame Brennier's breasts when she fell off her bicycle and her blouse split, and she hadn't been wearing a bra because everyone knew that French women didn't. Pongo wasn't sure if he believed it, but then it didn't really count because Madame Brennier was nearly sixty.

"I'd never seen a pair like that 'til I got here either!" shouted a particularly large man.

The lyre player's breasts shook as she joined the laughter sweeping through the glade. Pongo's face burned. "*Salveté,* sirs."

"Don't mind Achilles," shouted a man wearing the horsehair helmet of a Roman legionary. "He wouldn't have looked twice if he had!"

The large man laughed and threw an arm around the man next to him, who rested his bronze helmet on Achilles's shoulder.

"Give me a bedfellow like Patroclus any day," said Achilles. "He didn't hide from me for four days a month when we were alive, and joined me in Elysium now that we're dead. Show me the woman who could match that. But our new friend's gone purple!"

Achilles jumped to his feet and advanced on Pongo. "I'm not surprised you're a funny color under all that leather. Get rid of it, the sun never stops shining here."

Achilles grabbed Pongo's Mae West. Pongo flinched, but Achilles was undeterred. "What sort of armor is this? It's as soft as an empress's skirt! No wonder you joined us so young. What land are you from, young warrior?"

Pongo's buttocks clenched reflexively. "Britannia."

He unclipped his harness and dropped his parachute, dinghy, and Mae West to the ground. Achilles was right about the heat, and Pongo didn't want his help to undress.

The legionary leapt to his feet. "Britannia! I spent six years stuck on that pile of donkey droppings! We get no one new for a thousand years and now a Britaniculus! What next? A dog? A German?"

Pongo turned to the Roman's sneer. Anger burned away his embarrassment, and he wished Old Cribb had taught him some Latin expressions a bit more colorful than '*veni vidi vici*'.

"You impertinent man!" was the best he could do. He tried to bellow like the flight sergeant who'd taught him to march, but it sounded more like his attempt to sing the bass part of Bach's Requiem while his voice insisted on reverting to soprano.

The Roman was not intimidated. "Call me impertinent? I, a citizen of the greatest empire the world ever saw, am called impertinent by a tribe that paints itself blue?"

The insult to his country was the first thing that Pongo had understood since he died, and the wave of fury that swept through him brought the relief of a cold beer on a hot day. "Your little empire could fit into one little corner of His Britannic Majesty's! Look at a map of India some time!"

"Nonsense the pair of you," growled Achilles. "There was never an empire that could stand against my Myrmidons of Phthiotis."

"And all Greece was no more than a beetle's garden," Pongo said, delighted to hear his Latin getting more creative. "Glare at me if you like, you hairy tunic-lifter, but my king wouldn't use your kingdom as his lavatory!"

Pongo savored the awed expressions that surrounded him. People were actually backing away from his eloquence. That would teach them to remember they were only foreigners, heroes of the Trojan wars or not.

Achilles put out a hand and Patroclus placed a spear in it. Pongo's anger fell away as quickly as his parachute had. Achilles's eyes seized Pongo's as Patroclus buckled a shield on to his left arm.

Achilles advanced. Pongo backed away. It just wasn't fair that you could bring a spear with you but not a Spitfire. His foot caught on a Cypress root and he fell on his rear. Achilles put a foot on Pongo's parachute pack and raised his spear. "Now then boy, which of us pays homage to a piss-pot?" Achilles looked down at the pack. "What's that hissing noise?"

Pongo recognized his carbon dioxide cylinder. His dinghy leapt out of its pack, and Achilles disappeared under a sheet of yellow rubber.

Pongo sat up to see the lyrist looking back at him. She threw her head back and laughed as musically as she played the lyre. Then Pongo couldn't hear her any more because the whole glade quaked with laughter.

Patroclus's hands shook as he hauled the dinghy off Achilles, but even Achilles was laughing. "Thank Zeus Hector didn't have one of those!"

He wheeled on Pongo and hauled him into an embrace that nearly put him back on the ground. "Some ambrosia for Elysium's newest guest!"

The lyrist put her lyre aside and produced a clay urn from somewhere. She strolled toward him in a way that made Ingrid Bergman look as graceful as a cadet's first salute. She stopped in front of Pongo, and he forced himself to look up to her face. She nodded as though to say that he could go on looking if he wanted to. It occurred to Pongo that staring at the breasts of someone you hadn't been introduced to might constitute a gaffe. "My name's Pongo. How do you do?"

The lyrist held the urn to his lips. He almost took it before he remembered that the first drink always seemed harmless, but invariably put him on the path that ended in a blazing headache and a bill for broken furniture. "Oh no, not for me thank. . . ."

She pressed the urn between his lips, and a liquid that surpassed sweetness bathed his tongue. He decided that his new friends probably didn't pay subscriptions to the Temperance Society, and swallowed. The lyrist lowered the urn. Pongo found that she'd become even more desirable.

She kissed his lips. "My name is Pulchrissimé. I do very well, thank you."

A cheer engulfed them. Pulchrissimé placed her hands on his shoulders and pushed him to the ground. She straddled his midriff and caressed his face.

Pongo remembered Old Cribb catching some of the boys with a magazine full of grainy pictures of undressed women. Cold showers for the lot of them, followed by six of the best and one for luck.

He looked around to see the heroes of a thousand years of battles exchanging grins and laughs. "Um, Pulchrissimé, this is all rather sudden. . . ."

A finger over his lips silenced him. She kissed him again, and he decided that he'd spend the rest of eternity under a cold shower for one more kiss.

"Here he is!"

Pongo's lips froze on Pulchrissimé's.

"Ah, jolly good," replied another voice in English. Pongo didn't recognize the voice, but his spine prickled at the schoolmasterly inflection.

Pongo looked round as a tall man in a toga spoke to Pulchrissimé in the booming Latin of the first voice. "Get off him woman, he's a monotheist. These fools," he gestured at a small man sporting a tweed jacket and a pointed beard, "sent him here by mistake."

Pulchrissimé jumped off Pongo as though he was a wasp nest. "A monotheist! But I kissed him!"

She hawked and spat.

The warriors' grins dropped away and Pongo saw the Roman fingering the pommel of his sword.

The tweed jacketed man held up his hands. "I'm terribly sorry my dear. We get so many these days that we're bound to lose track of a few. We do our best, you know."

"Well do better," boomed the man in the toga. He pointed at Pulchrissimé. "And you had better take a bath immediately."

The bearded man pulled Pongo to his feet. "Oh dear, poor Hades gets so upset about these things," he said in English, apparently oblivious to the angry murmur swelling around them. "But really, we haven't lost anyone down here since the Black Death. You *are* Pilot Officer WR Ponsonby, five-oh-nine-two-one-oh?"

Pongo tried to assume the pose that seemed to work for the judges, but couldn't stop himself hanging his head as he had on the day he had to explain how astonished he was that his initials had carved themselves into a school desk. "Yes."

"Well that's a relief. I'd have some explaining to do if I came back with the wrong man. I'm Mephistopheles, by the way," he pumped Pongo's limp hand. "Aha, I see you've heard of me. I expect you're surprised to see me doing this job, but we're all rather rushed these days and we do our bit where we can. There is a war on, you know."

Pongo felt sick. Years of church instruction and he'd crashed on his first solo, but this was far worse than bending a Tiger Moth. Half an hour away from teachers and superior officers and he'd been fighting, drinking, and fornicating. Now here was the demon that tempted Faust to take him to task for it. An eternity of cold showers was the best he could expect.

Mephistopheles rattled on. "Just a quick shout on the *wireless,* I think you chaps call it, and it's chocks away."

Mephistopheles took Pongo's arm and turned him around to face another pane of dark glass that had appeared from nowhere. Pongo found himself practically frog marched through it before he could say a word.

"Here we are, home at last and sorry about the detour," said Mephistopheles. "How d'you like it? Um, I don't mean to presume, but you'd find it easier to express an informed opinion if you opened your eyes."

Pongo took a tentative breath, and the pleasantly warm air persuaded him to open an eye. He expected to receive a red-hot needle in it, but all he saw was blue sky over white clouds.

Clouds. Sky. Nothing under his feet. His hand leapt for where his ripcord should be, but got a handful of silk robe. He didn't seem to be falling toward the clouds, so he looked down and saw why. He was standing on them. He took an experimental step and found himself walking across the cloud, though he could feel nothing beneath his bare feet.

Pongo turned to Mephistopheles, but the small man had already left.

"Ponsonby Minor? *C'est pas possible!*"

Pongo looked up and rubbed his eyes. It made no difference. The woman looking at him still had a faint nimbus of light over her brown hair.

She spoke in rapid French, and smiled at his blank expression. "Ah, but you never did pay attention to our beautiful language," she said in English. "But how did you come to be here? I don't remember seeing you in the chapel."

"I'm sorry," he said. "Have we met?"

Pongo scrutinized the woman's face. Her features were unremarkable, but they had a sort of purity, as though every blemish had been cleansed away. Pongo was sure he would have remembered such a face if he'd seen it before.

The woman opened her hands. "But surely you remember my voice, even if you don't recognize my face, *mon jeune brave.*"

Pongo sat down with a force that would have bruised his tailbone if there had been anything solid to bruise it on. "Madame Brennier?"

"*Oui, c'est moi. J'ai* . . . but you never did pay attention in my lessons, did you? Even after I separated you from the Harris boy. I look thirty years younger than you remember of course. I was in church so much *more* when I was young, but what can you have to confess when you are nearly sixty and live in *England?*" she smiled. "But what are you doing here? I thought you were C of E?"

"Well, I. . . ."

"C of E?" Mephistopheles's voice cut off Pongo's reply. "Don't be ridiculous! He converted last year, didn't you old boy?" Mephistopheles clapped Pongo's back. "Sorry to break up the reunion, but I need to borrow the man of the hour. Some forms to fill in before you get too settled.

Frightful bore and all that, but needs must."

Madame Brennier genuflected and Mephistopheles pulled Pongo to his feet for the second time in ten minutes. He leaned toward him confidentially. "You didn't say anything about not being Catholic, did you?"

"I didn't really get a chance to say anything."

"Good, good, they've thought they've had the place to themselves for the last thousand years, it wouldn't do to disillusion them. Now, as for you. Frankly, it's a bit embarrassing to have misplaced you twice. Of course, we're all at sixes and sevens with the war, but you *have* been rather unlucky."

Mephistopheles's eyebrows pressed together, making him look more like a schoolmaster than ever. "What I mean is, the *headmaster* would like to see you in person. Hear *your side,* so to speak."

"The headmaster? You mean. . . ."

"Yes."

Pongo stammered as his meager social graces screamed inadequacy at him. "But I haven't a thing to wear!"

"You're fine as you are. Just call him sir and don't slouch."

Mephistopheles spun Pongo around into a pane of dark glass that had appeared behind them. Pongo didn't know what to expect on the other side, but found that he and Mephistopheles were simply floating in, well, nothing. It was neither cold nor warm and he could feel nothing supporting him, but he had no sensation of falling.

"Here we are," said Mephistopheles.

"But there's nothing here."

"There will be. Sorry must dash. Someone's sent a whole U-boat crew to the Zoroastrians. Ta-ta."

Pongo looked around to see that Mephistopheles had already vanished, but that order was appearing in the nothing. It was wrapping and folding itself into a dark face with a black beard and a turban.

Nothing reverberated to the clearing of an enormous throat and the words, "*Salaam aleikhum.*"

Pongo forced himself to speak. "How do you do?"

The dark eyes widened. "Are you of the faithful? You are very strangely dressed."

"People keep telling me that. Sir."

Pongo heard another voice, although he couldn't make out the words. The face rolled its eyes. "Oh, not again."

The skin lightened and became a little ruddy, while the dark beard faded to gray. The turban sank into a crop of thinning gray hair. The new face had an air of experience and wisdom that did remind Pongo of his headmaster, though his headmaster had never started an interview by changing color.

"I do apologize," said the voice in an accent that matched the new face. "One meets so many people these days that One is forever making these *faux pas*. I do my best, but no one's infallible."

"Not at all. Don't mention it, sir."

"Now what are we to do with you? You've seen far more of our premises than you're supposed to, but it was hardly your fault. To misplace you once may be regarded as misfortune. To misplace you twice seems like carelessness. I say, didn't somebody say something like that before?"

"Oscar Wilde wasn't it, sir?"

"Oh yes. Well at least you didn't see where we put *him*. Now then, do you have any preferences yourself?"

"Well sir, I must admit that I'm rather confused. I mean, how do things work here?"

"Ah now, that would be a bit complicated. I really haven't got time to explain a system that's taken seven hundred millennia to put together."

The indistinct voice floated through nothing again.

"Well tell them to wait," snapped the face. "Honestly," he said to Pongo, "it's been like this ever since you people got it into your heads that you wanted to talk to me directly. Never a moment's peace. Why you can't make do with the demigods and avatars like you used to is beyond me. What else are they for?"

"Wouldn't that be idolatry, sir?"

"Call it what you like, it makes my day easier. When people first got the idea that they were too good for demigods, I sent them mad to try to put them off the idea. Gracious me, look what I did to Job! Much good it did."

A sigh ruffled Pongo's hair.

"I'm even more confused now," said Pongo.

The voice took on a hint of compassion. "Yes, of course you are. I'd forgotten that you English assume I was born in Berkshire and went to school at Eton. I should have seen this coming a couple of hundred years ago. It was a mistake to let the industrial revolution start in a country that thinks Yorkshire pudding is the height of good cuisine and that fornication is a sin."

"Sir?"

"Well, Yorkshire pudding's hardly the best the world has to offer, is it? We've got a program to get you English to take yourselves less seriously, but it won't really get going for another twenty years or so. If only I'd thought of John Lennon at the same time I thought of Queen Victoria."

"John who?"

The distant voice spoke again.

"I'm being as quick as I can! If you hadn't lost him, this conversation wouldn't be necessary!"

The voice resumed its conversational tone. "Apparently there's a queue building up, so we'd better make haste. The point is, where would you like to go?"

"I don't know sir. I'm just so confused. All my life, I've believed that you, well, that you looked like this all the time."

"Quite so. If certain creations had been doing their jobs, you would still believe it and much embarrassment would have been spared. However, I think the choice really ought to be yours, under the irregular circumstances."

This was worse than waking up to the ferryman. Pongo had never felt less able to make a decision in his life, or since. An idea struck him. "Can you tell me where Harry Harris is, sir? He bought it last week."

The face raised its voice. "Harry Harris? You hear that?"

The other voice replied, and the face grimaced. "Oh my word, they've done it again!"

"Sir?"

"I'm afraid your friend was mislaid as well. He was sent to the Hindus."

"The Hindus?"

"Yes, he seems to have got himself reincarnated."

"Sir?"

"They sent him back as a deep sea squid. He died in a fire didn't he? It seems they decided he deserves to be kept well away from the stuff this time round."

"A squid? Harry's turned into a squid?"

"Yes. He won't be too bright of course, but no one who went to your school would notice the difference."

Pongo liked swimming. "Can squid get confused and miserable over theology?"

"Not at all. They don't have expensive enough educations."

"Then I'd like to join him, if I may."

The face relaxed into a smile. "Good. That's settled then. Have a good time."

Pongo opened his mouth to say thank you, but a splash of salt water stilled the words, and he found himself unable to think about anything beyond getting out of his egg case and snatching a copepod in his gangling young tentacles.

~

A version of this story was originally published in the webzine Kenoma.

D.J. Cockburn *has been listening to a long monologue of rejection slips for several years now, in between earning a living through medical research on various parts of the African continent. Oh yes, and publishing the occasional story, most recently in the* Warrior Wisewoman 2 *anthology by Norilana Books.*

Windows to the Soul

Gerri Leen

She sits down at the bar, her tanned skin gleaming in a way her eyes do not. She orders a highball from Mort, and he moves away to make the drink, not looking over to see his reflection. But she watches him go and as she turns back, she catches a glimpse of herself in me and stops.

She stares and I taste. She's a deep one. Not much happiness for how pretty she is. Lots of pain. And regret—regret seasons everything so beautifully. I want to hold onto this one.

Mort carries the drink over when he could have just slid it down the bar. He stands between us, breaking the connection, and the taste of her is gone.

I hate Mort a lot of the time. I know he hates me, too.

"Why don't you take one of the booths in the back," he says.

"I'm fine here." She smiles; it's a tight smile.

"They're much more comfortable."

"I said I was fine here." Now she sounds mad. And I could clue Mort in —if I had the ability to speak—that trying to strong-arm her is the wrong way to get her to do something.

"Suit yourself." He sounds defeated, and she glances at him as if she can't figure out why he cares.

She doesn't get up, and Mort sneaks a look at me, in that way he has where he can see me but not himself. It's a way he's perfected over the years of our partnership. He bought the bar knowing what I was—what I do. He knows the profits are in large part due to me calling people in. Those who plonk themselves down at his bar are tired of pain, and they don't mind the idea of having it sucked right out of them—even if there'll be nothing left once it's gone. Even though they'll wander out of the bar, and get in their cars, and drive off the road into a tree or a ditch or right off the mountain if they get that far. Most of them don't get that far. Most of them I drain nearly dry.

One time I took too much and the person died on the stool. That was before Mort, back when Jimmy owned the bar. Jimmy was furious with me for that. Covered me up for a month and wouldn't let me drink anyone, even though the bar was barely pulling in enough to meet expenses without me bringing people in. The bar doesn't have many regulars, and those that come know something's off, but they don't know it's me.

Once, though, back in Jimmy's day, one of the customers did figure it out. He came back in the night, tried to shatter me with a ball-peen hammer. I don't shatter. And if you touch me with your bare hands, I can take you. He was careful not to look, but he was lax about the touching. No one ever saw him again.

Jimmy must have told Mort not to touch me when he explained about the bar, because Mort always wears gloves when he cleans me. Not that I need that much cleaning. The energy going in and out keeps me fresh.

Keeps the bar fresh, too. Fresh faces, fresh pain.

The woman looks up at me again, and she thinks she's staring into her own eyes, but really she's staring into mine.

"Where you from?" Mort asks.

She answers as if she's a million miles away—and she is, she's inside me. "Dallas."

"Long way from home."

She shrugs. Her reflection does the same, but if she paid close attention, she'd notice the reflected eyes don't mirror hers, anymore. They're fixed on her. Even when she blinks, her reflected eyes don't—I don't let them. A meal like this, you don't leave in the middle of.

"Gotta be people that care about you," Mort says, and I know what he's doing. He's tried this before, and sometimes it works. Sometimes he can talk them out of me. Out of death.

But not very often. You don't hear my call unless you're on the ledge.

"Nobody cares about me."

Hard to believe no one cares about a pretty girl like her. But the energy in her mind is zipping in ways that's not quite sane, and it colors her view of everything. My dinner's a little crazy, but that only makes her taste better to me.

"What's your name?" Mort has always needed to know who my victims are. In the safe in the back room, he has a book where he writes down their names like it's some kind of memorial. If the cops ever raid the joint, he's going to be in a heap of trouble.

Not me, though. I'll survive. Always do. I've been around a long time and don't plan on leaving. Can't remember a time when I wasn't here. Can't remember where I come from or how I came to be. Doesn't really matter to me. I feed. That's what I do.

I feed. They die.

Mort's not giving up. "You gotta have a name."

She looks away from me, and I feel the separation echoing through my entire essence. "My name's Debbie."

"Nice name. I'm Mort." He holds his hand out, and I want to kill him. He's trying to get her planted back in their reality. Get her to connect with life and him, not with me.

She closes her eyes, then she opens them and it looks like she wants to cry. "Maybe I will sit in one of those booths." She slides off the barstool, and the connection between us breaks with a stinging snap.

"Next round's on the house." Mort throws me one of his looks of triumph. His eyes don't meet mine, of course.

He's won this time. But there'll be others. There are always others.

He can't win them all.

~

Gerri Leen *lives in Northern Virginia and originally hails from Seattle. She came to fiction writing late in life and writes stories in many genres, including fantasy—both light and dark, and often centered around mythology—science fiction, and literary. She dabbles in poetry and is co-editing* Renaissance Festival Tales, *a fantasy anthology. In addition to* Triangulation: Dark Glass, *look for her stories in such places as:* Sword and Sorceress 23, Return to Luna, Triangulation: Taking Flight, Footprints, Sails & Sorcery, Desolate Places, *and* GlassFire. *Visit http://www.gerrileen.com to see what else she's been up to.*

More Things in Heaven and Earth

Jason K. Chapman

"How, exactly, do you plan to kill God?" The colonel stared at the scientist as he pulled himself down to the table. His hand gripped the table's edge, holding him against the freefall drift.

Hovering by the room's hatch, hands lightly clasping the grip bar behind him, Horatio Judison watched the two men face off across the table. As the colonel's attaché, his job was to watch, wait, and listen. The scientist bobbed at the end of a short safety tether. His name was Gunther and he was supposed to be the salvation of the colony on Danika.

"Not God, *per se*." Gunther's hands fluttered nervously. His tether went taut and he bounced back toward the conference table. He clearly had little experience in freefall. "All gods, really. You see, it's not about killing gods so much as destroying faith."

The colonel peered at the device strapped to the middle of the table. "Well, you must have something, otherwise the Central Authority wouldn't have shipped you all the way from Earth, but I'll be damned if I believe this little box will do the trick."

A pleasant pinging sound floated through the air—the five minute notice before their shuttle dropped toward the planet. Judison noticed the quick darting movement of the scientist's eyes. He was hiding something.

"You're the expert, Lieutenant Judison. What do you think?" The colonel cocked his head and smiled. "Do you think, after all we've been through, that we can finally undo the CDS with the flick of a switch?"

Judison doubted it. No group that dedicated, that certain, that *faithful*, could be destroyed so easily. He envied them their clarity, though he took great care to hide it; any hint of enemy influence would wreck his career. "I'm hardly an expert, sir. The abstract Mister Gunther provided held very little detail."

"I'm not talking about the device and you know it!" The colonel held his scowl on Judison for several breaths. When he finally turned back to Gunther, it disappeared, replaced by an oil smooth smile. "Lieutenant Judison, here—that is, Horatio Judison naGloria, clansmen are very conscious of their clan histories—lived among the Children of the Dying Sun for several years. He was an *agent provocateur,* as they say. In short, a spy. He was completely immersed in their culture and teachings. Isn't that so, Lieutenant?"

He waited for a response. Judison refused him even a nod.

The colonel turned back to Gunther. "It's a wonder, after so much time being subjected to the cult, that every test and interview indicates that he wasn't won over by them—that he's completely loyal to the Defense Force and the Colonial Authority."

Gunther, clearly aware that there was something going on beneath the simple chatter, looked around the room nervously. "Astounding."

"Yes, it is." The colonel smiled broadly. "One might almost say 'unbelievable.'"

Judison gritted his teeth. It wasn't the first time he'd suffered the colonel's insinuations. His assignment to the colonel had been forced on them both just over three months before, and neither of them had ever been comfortable with it. Maybe it was unbelievable that he hadn't been turned, but a whole herd of brain pickers from the medical corps had stampeded through his head and they all agreed: Judison believed in the mission as much as he ever had. And that was the rub. Judison himself couldn't say how much he believed, or if he ever had. Having seen the Children up close, he knew what belief looked like. He just wasn't sure he knew what it felt like.

Gunther cleared his throat. "I understand the cult is quite compelling."

"Religion," Judison said.

"Excuse me?"

Judison nodded to Gunther. "It's a religion, not a cult."

The colonel scowled, studying Judison's face. "What difference does that make?"

Careful to keep his face impassive, Judison held the colonel's gaze. The rumor mill said it had been the colonel's idea to use an undercover agent to blow up the Children's leadership. Judison had been chosen for the mission for both his military experience and his clan background. Having grown up with the traditions and structure of the clans, the Colonial Authority reasoned, would make him better able to fit in with the Children. Judison turned back to Gunther. "You can kill a cult by cutting off its head."

The scientist nodded enthusiastically. "That's the beauty of my device. Cult or religion doesn't matter. Without followers, neither can survive."

The colonel seemed reluctant to take his eyes off of Judison, but he finally turned back to the device. The drop warning pinged the one minute notice. "Go on," he said.

"The brain is highly modular." Gunther pulled himself along the table to the nearest drop chair. He eased into it, reaching for the straps. "Different sections handle different functions. That's a gross over-simplification, of course, because some of the more subtle functions require activity in several sections at once, and some areas can learn new functions in order to route around damage, but—"

"Skip the details, Mister Gunther!" The colonel glowered at the scientist as if he were a raw recruit. In Judison's experience, the colonel didn't like to sully himself with details. He liked his instruments blunt. "What does it do?"

"Abstract thought." Gunther scrambled to buckle his safety harness when the triple gong of the drop alert sounded. The shuttle gave a slight nudge and that was all. He looked embarrassed, talking faster. "Specifically, abstract thought that isn't based on a known referential framework. You see, normally the prefrontal cortex operates in concert with both the long- and short-term memory, mapping possible outcomes against known experiences, but once the brain makes the leap to faith, everything changes. One tiny area of the amygdala lights up, enabling abstractions beyond known possibilities. I call it the God Module."

Judison pushed himself toward the drop chair at the near end of the table. He checked his watch. It was less than ten minutes before the first retro burn. Though he pretended not to, he noticed the colonel's wary glance. He could feel the man's distrust. If the colonel knew the truth about Judison's last day among the Children, he'd shoot Judison without a moment's hesitation.

"That's it?" The colonel moved to strap himself in. "That's what makes them religious zealots?"

Judison winced. He covered it by cinching his shoulder straps tighter. The Children weren't zealots. Who cared what they believed? Maybe the star of Bethlehem really *had* been a supernova. Maybe billions of beings really *had* died to spread their enlightened atoms across the galaxy. Judison didn't care about the scriptural details. What mattered was that the Children had a star to steer by. They didn't have to founder in a sea of second guesses, the way he did. They just knew which way to go.

Gunther shook his head. "Zealotry is a far more complicated affair— more psychological than neurological. No, to put it simply, exposure to this device scrambles one's ability to have faith."

"Come again?" The colonel paused in the middle of buckling his harness. "How in the world can it do that?"

Gunther seemed surprised by the question. "Why, by destroying the neuronal connections to the God Module, of course."

Judison pretended to adjust his harness again. He'd seen pulsed maser weapons. He'd used subsonic wavefront generators in riot control. He'd fired just about every kind of projectile weapon on Danika. This thing looked like none of them. It looked innocuous, like office equipment. He smiled at the idea that he would have to take its capabilities on faith.

"Something funny, Lieutenant?" The colonel glared at him. Judison could feel the man's distrust wash over him like a hot desert wind.

"No, sir." Judison shrugged. "I just don't believe it."

"You have to believe it." Gunther blinked at him. "It's science."

A quiet smile on his face, the colonel turned back to Gunther. "What's its range?"

"Well, ordinarily, we'd focus it through a wave guide and tune the signal to the subject's approximate brain mass."

"The range!"

Gunther jerked back, startled. "A hundred meters, maybe, at full power, but I can't—"

A new tone sounded from the ceiling—five minutes to retro burn.

"Turn it on," the colonel said. He looked calmly at Judison.

Gunther sputtered. "No, you don't understand. We can't just—"

"Turn it on!" Without looking away from Judison, the colonel tapped a finger on the table. "If any CDS spies made it through security screening, I want to at least make it hard on them."

Gunther looked frightened. "You don't understand, if we—"

The colonel cut him off by drawing his sidearm. "Now."

Hands shaking, his eyes wide and darting, Gunther pressed a sequence of controls on the device. Several lights on the panel came to life. He sat back, still staring at the colonel's pistol. "It's on."

Judison thought he felt a tingling sensation between his eyes, but he might have been imagining it. He stared at the colonel as the final retro warning sounded. Did he feel any different? What about his thoughts? Was the colonel still a bloodthirsty ass? Yes. Was the Danika Security Force still obsessed with control at any cost? Yes. Were the Children right in their beliefs? Were they justified in their fight for freedom and independence? Judison sighed. That was no help. He hadn't had an answer to that *before* the device went hot.

The colonel looked around, seeming confused. It took him three tries to holster is weapon. "Is it on? I don't understand. How can this thing even work? Are you sure it's on?"

"Of course it's on!" Gunther's petulant tone probably passed for sternness in scientific circles. "The lights are on, aren't they?"

Judison felt the shuttle jitter as it descended into the planet's outer atmosphere. That wasn't right. The burn should have happened before they touched air. He checked his watch. Retro fire was already a minute late. He slapped the release on his harness and jumped for the hatch.

"I knew it!" The colonel's voice roared from behind him. "You went over, didn't you? Didn't you?"

Judison pulled himself into the corridor, but something caught his leg. He looked back to find the colonel. He had one hand clamped on Judison's ankle and the other on the hatchway.

"You can't escape, Judison! There's no escape."

Judison tried to shake free, but the colonel's grip tightened. "Sir, the burn is late. Something's wrong."

"I'll say something's wrong."

"We're drilling in. Let me go!"

"You can't know that." The colonel tugged him back toward the hatch. "You're lying."

Judison slammed his free foot into the man's jaw. The vice came off of his ankle. Without looking back, he tugged himself down the corridor toward the cockpit. The guide rail shook under his hand. He could see the ship vibrating around him. By the time he reached the cockpit hatch, he could barely hold on. He swung the hatch open and dove in.

"Tell him!" The copilot was out of his seat, pressing himself against the com station. He looked at Judison pleadingly. "Tell him it's not supposed to shake like this. He *has* to push the button."

Judison leapt to where the pilot sat frozen in his seat. He glanced at the board. Hull temperature warnings. Mass proximity alert. Delta-V alarms. The ship was screaming for help. He reached for the booster trigger, but the pilot batted his hand away.

"Don't do that!" Twisting in his seat, the pilot tried to push Judison back. "Fuel burns! How do you know it won't just explode and blow us all to hell?"

Judison gave the pilot a left jab, dazing him. "Because it never has before."

He strapped himself into the copilot's seat.

"That's not true." The copilot was clutching the back of the seat. "It has happened before."

"Not when I was on board." Judison slapped the retro trigger. Gee forces shoved him into his seat. They were way off the curve. At the current rate, he wouldn't be able to lose enough speed to deploy the wings until it was too late. Blinded by ionized atmosphere, the screens were useless. The computer could only give him best guesses based on the last known data.

It was simple. They were going to die. Part of Judison knew that. That's where it got confusing, because he couldn't believe it. He'd never died before. Others had, of course, but not Horatio Judison naGloria. To the best of his knowledge, the Gloria clan would live forever in the eldest son of Judi.

Fact: The shuttle was twenty percent over safe-rated speed for wing deployment. Fact: If he couldn't slow them down, they'd crash. Fact: Without the wings, he'd never slow the shuttle down to a safe landing speed. Fact: He'd never seen anyone rip the wings off a shuttle before. It seemed possible, even likely, but he couldn't bring himself to believe it.

Judison slammed the wing release lever home.

Metal screamed through the hull as gee forces crushed the air from Judison's lungs. New alarms sprang up on the board. The shuttle fought like a wild animal as he wrestled for control. He got the nose up, belly flat to the thickening air. More alarms went off as the wings bowed back and primary hydraulics failed. Judison shrugged. It was better than a brick, but worse than a glider. He tried to coax some s-turns out of the shuttle to shed as much speed as possible. She responded stubbornly, but she responded.

At last, with his altitude still bleeding away too fast, he lined up an approach in the eastern limb of the Maleth Desert. The whole area was under CDS control. As interesting as the landing was going to be, what happened afterward was likely to be even more so. He had no choice but to deliver them all into the hands of the Children.

Judison watched the ground rush toward him. It looked to be more sand than rock. He angled the lift-assist thrusters as far forward as possible and kicked them on full, then braced himself. When they clipped the top of the first shallow dune, the nose lurched skyward. He caught the next one with the tail. Judison slammed against the safety harness as the ship flipped forward. The copilot flew over Judison's shoulder. Something slammed the back of his head and everything went dark.

The copilot was dead. Neck broken, his body was draped across the control panel like a rag doll. The pilot was alive, but unconscious. Judison blinked in the dim glow of emergency lights. The control panel was completely dark. Staggering against the awkward tilt of the deck, he went to check out what was left of the shuttle.

A hot wind blew out of the conference room hatchway. He found a huge gash ripped through the hull, most likely peeled off with the left wing. Surprisingly, both Gunther and the colonel were alive, their chairs still welded firmly to the deck. The table had ripped loose and was lodged in the hole in the hull.

"You did this." The colonel unclipped his harness. "Didn't you?"

Raw sunlight streamed in from the desert, glinting off of Gunther's machine where it sat, still strapped to the table top. Lights blinked on its control panel. Judison rubbed at the tingle in his forehead. "If I'd wanted us all dead, I'd have stayed in my seat."

Gunther tried to get up, but fell back, whimpering.

The colonel eased his sidearm out of its holster. "It's part of your plan. Sacrifice yourself. I knew they'd gotten to you. Knew it!"

Judison held his hands away from his body. "That was your plan, Colonel, remember? I was supposed to blow up the CDS leadership even if it meant blowing myself up too."

The colonel's aim firmed up on Judison's chest. "You're working for *them* now."

"No, Colonel." Slowly, Judison slid into the nearest chair. "But I'm not really working for you, either. Tell me something. What makes you so sure the Defense Force is right?"

"I don't care!"

"No?" Judison kept his voice calm. "How do you know you're doing the right thing?"

Some of the anger washed out of the colonel's face. What replaced it looked a little like doubt. "I follow orders."

"Of course you do. You always have." Judison gave the colonel a sympathetic smile. He understood the man, now, even if the man didn't understand himself. "We all did. But are you sure they're right? Are you sure the Colonial Authority is right? Do you *know* it?"

"This is . . . they've always. . . ." The pistol wavered as the colonel shook his head. "It's that damn machine. Shut it off!"

Gently, slowly, Judison stood. He kept his hands at his sides. "Too late, Colonel. The damage is done."

"I have my orders."

"But you've always believed they were right. You had faith that your superiors knew the right thing to do, didn't you? You didn't have to know, you just had to believe."

"No!" Still holding the pistol, the colonel pressed his hands against his head. "How can they know they're right? How can anyone? We've been fighting since before I was born—before *they* were born. How can they know?"

"It's hard, I know." Judison moved within arm's reach. "It happened to me while I was with the Children. That's why I blew my own cover. That's why I had to fight my way out when your backup agent tried to stop me. I saw what belief looked like—saw it up close. I saw what it meant when people knew they were right. And I knew I wasn't one of them."

The colonel dropped his hands. They hung limp at his sides. The pistol dangled loosely, as if forgotten. "This doesn't make any sense."

"None of it does." Judison took the weapon from the colonel's unresisting hand. "Do you see, now? Do you see?"

The colonel searched Judison's face, seeming not to find what he was looking for. "You couldn't believe anymore."

"No." Staring at the weapon in his hand, Judison shrugged. "Without that, I had nothing."

"So what do we do?"

"We start over. Figure it out." Judison shoved the pistol into his belt. "Then we do what makes sense."

Nodding, the colonel squatted down next to Gunther's machine. His finger traced its dull metal edge. "Then we spread the word."

~

Jason K. Chapman *lives in New York City where he works as the IT Director for Poets & Writers. He is the author of the cyber-thriller* The Heretic *and his short fiction has appeared in* Cosmos Magazine, Jim Baen's Universe, Andromeda Spaceways Inflight Magazine, *and others. You can learn more at his Web site: jasonkchapman.com.*

On the Path

Kelly A. Harmon

The soul-powered plow halted mid-furrow and hastened to a shuddering stop as the reincarnation engine seized up.

"Not again," said Tân, swinging his legs to the side of the wooden tank and jumping down out of the seat. As he stepped forward to check the soul-seal, the cap fired off with a hollow thud, like a cork from a jug.

Thick white steam, more creamy than translucent, escaped the ruptured tank with a shrill whistle, erupting geyser-straight into the air until a strong gust of north wind blew it toward Zhourong. Tân could almost hear the screams of the souls in the din.

"*Ma-de!*" he said, pulling off his gloves and slapping them on the tank. "Curse you to hell if you touch my wife or children!" he shouted to the escaping vapor. "Leave them alone or I'll kill you the moment you're reborn!"

Thank the gods the steaming cloud moved toward town and away from his home. The south wind had blown the last time this happened. He remembered that time well: both his wife and two teenage daughters became pregnant that night. His youngest child was eight, his two grandchildren the same age, all born only days apart.

That accident brought both joy and pain. Three more mouths to feed indebted him to the temple, for he could not pay his promised offerings on time. Yet he'd been blessed with more children, and grandchildren, who would grow up together. And he'd been compensated with larger herds. He'd earned two additional milch cows, several twins of sheep—doubling the flock—and the chickens destined for the soup pot all laid eggs the very same night. He'd siphoned the souls off those eggs after cracking them for breakfast the next morning.

But those souls had been infantile and had powered his reincarnation engine for less than a year.

These souls he'd worked more than eight years—they were not young like the others. They'd spent time in the engines for which they should be compensated on their journey to Tao. What happened to escaped souls after spending eight years on the path of reincarnation? He was certain he didn't want to know.

Tân looked back at the ruptured tank. It's silk-smooth sides and dark, oiled wood denoted many years of loving use and care. Could he forget about it? Ignore the tank breach and continue as if nothing had happened? He'd have to revert back to manual farming . . . and Heng and his daughters would have to join him in the fields. He shook his head. I don't want it to come to that, he thought. Yet, he didn't know if he could do this a second time.

The north wind blew again, cutting though the high collar of his quilted tunic and Tân shivered. He plucked his bamboo hat off and ran a calloused hand through greying black strands escaped from his waist-length queue and walked to the mudbrick cabin he shared with his wife, daughters and grandchildren.

Yes, he could do this again: admit the failure of the tank to the priests, start once more with a new batch of souls. . . . It was easier than asking his family to help.

Mud sucked at his clogs as Tân neared his home. He'd reserved the driest section of land for the grain fields, and as a result, the house wallowed in mud in the rainy season. To compensate, Tân had raised the building up and built a wrapping porch around all four sides of it. In the summer, he and his family slept outside upon the wide deck, in much more spacious comfort than their tiny rooms allowed.

He walked up the four steps to the porch, kicked off his shoes, and stepped over the raised sill of the door before entering the house.

"Heng?" he called, pushing in the wooden door.

She looked up from the steaming pot of rice on the brick stove.

"*Ai?*" She smiled, settling the lid back on the pot and walking toward Tân. She halted at his next words.

"We have need of a priest," he said. "The tank on the reincarnation engine burst again."

Heng moved her hands to her womb, pressing against it, as if to block entry.

"The wind is blowing north," he said. "You have nothing to worry about."

Slowly, Heng lowered her hands, as if not quite believing. She looked to the tiny, crowded altar in a small alcove in the rear of the house. "Shall we. . . ?"

"Yes, of course," he said. "There's no sense jinxing our luck."

He walked to the altar and bowed, then lifted three new sticks of incense, lit them from a ceremonial candle and placed them in a burner.

Without being asked, Heng gathered together a sack of tangerines for Tân to take as an offering to the temple.

Tân bowed toward the altar again, then met Heng at the door. "I won't be gone long," he said, taking the sack.

Tân climbed the mountain to the temple.

Compared to the Bogda Feng, this mountain was a hillock, but knowing that didn't make the climb any easier. *Old Grandfather,* he prayed to the father of all gods, *I understand the need for the privacy of those who serve the Gods, but could not this privacy be found on less steep ground?*

Then he saw the red-headed crane, a sign of luck, and immortality. He bowed to the crane, and continued. Perhaps Old Grandfather sent him a sign by way of the bird.

The temple abutted the mountain face on a narrow plateau near a narrow, rapid stream. A slender footbridge, painted red with yellow lotus blossoms and hung with tiny brass bells arched over the small stream and deposited those who crossed to within a few feet of the temple.

Tân could see that the rice-paper door of the temple stood wide. Three priests sat cross-legged on the porch in a bit of watery sunshine. Eyes closed, they breathed as one, hands in their laps, clasped in *Zhen's Supplication.* Inside the temple, a free-standing altar squatted behind them, wisps of burning incense whorling to the ceiling.

The smell of honeysuckle, his favorite blossom, reached Tân before he set foot on the bridge. Smiling, he decided the monk's choice of incense must be, like the crane, another sign of good luck.

Tân walked across the bridge, bells jangling with each step, discordant in the quiet of the mountainside. Below, the current sang over the rocks, peaceful in comparison to the clangor of the bells.

He stopped on the other side and bowed, waiting for the priests to acknowledge him.

"Only those seeking favors climb the mountain bearing gifts," said first-priest Sheng. She lifted a mask at her side, and donned the face of the Jade Emperor who sits in judgment in heaven: his eyes and ears larger than life in order to see and hear all he needs to know.

Tân bowed, shucked his clogs and stepped onto the porch. "My soul tank has ruptured again. I need to purchase additional souls."

"You have awful luck with reincarnation engines," Sheng said, "Perhaps you should consider a more traditional mode of farming." She lowered the mask.

"I have considered it," said Tân, "but—"

"But what about your donations to the temple?" she asked. Beside her, Li and Hu nodded their heads.

Hu said, "Your crops would be smaller, and you might still give thirty percent to the temple. But thirty percent of a reduced donation will slow your path to salvation. . . ." He drew a line in the sandy floor with a black, lacquered nail filed to a precise point. "The paths of your wife and children, too."

Li stood, donning the mask of Guan Yin and taking the position of *Guan's Hauteur:* one hand on her chin, the other clasping the upraised elbow. "You have grandchildren, too, do you not, Tân?" she asked. "Have your daughters married yet?"

She relaxed the position and tugged a carved, jade barrette from her topknot, letting loose a cascade of hair that nearly touched the saffron-yellow embroidery on the hem of her purple robes.

Tân felt anger growing in his chest. This was not the conversation he'd come to have. He'd come to buy souls and get back to the fields. He hadn't time to discuss the philosophy of Tao.

They knew he'd chosen to farm wheat and barley because it was harder than flooding his fields and wallowing in rice like every other farmer. His uncommon crops yielded enough money to buy his way past the lower stages of salvation. And if Old Grandfather willed it, the paths of his entire family. His methods were not just self-serving, he hoped to smooth the way for them all. Is that not what a father does for his children?

He closed his eyes.

Grandfather, he prayed, *please see me through this trial with money enough to skip ahead on the path to Tao. And please grant me the ability to remain calm in your temple, among your most ardent followers.*

He opened his eyes.

Grandfather willing, he and his family would spend no time in the soul tanks. Years in a reincarnation engine only to be expelled in a single steaming overload into the belly of a nearby cow, or gods forfend, the belly of a chicken—only to be plucked, boiled, eaten and tossed back on a lower path to begin again—that wasn't for him! He could afford to be above that. He'd worked hard and given much.

Wasn't he willing to sacrifice luxuries he could well afford to secure a place in the Tao that much sooner?

He thought, *I have scrimped like a millet farmer, worn patched pants, fed my family the meals of a less prosperous man, so to make the path to heaven shorter for my family.* Surely, with his work and his money, they could make themselves a place on a higher plane when they died in this lifetime.

Calmness, Grandfather, he thought again.

He turned to Li. "Of course my daughters have not married, honorable one," he said. "Who would have them now?" He bowed over his hat, clasped between his hands.

"You regret their burden?" asked Hu.

"I want them happy," Tân said.

"And out of your house," Sheng said.

Tân stepped back, stricken, almost out of the small temple. His anger fled.

"It's not like that, honorable one," he said. "I would welcome a son-in-law in my home."

"Unusual," said Hu.

"But not unheard of," said Tân. "My home is large enough. The land can support more."

"And sons-in-law could work the land, bring in more income . . . allowing you to bypass many more stages of reincarnation on the way to Tao," Sheng said.

"It's allowed," said Tân. A crackle rose up from the brim of his hat, now crushed in his hands.

"But only if you realize what you're giving up," said Sheng.

"I do, honorable one," Tân said, bowing. "Hard work, discomfort, prolonged journey."

"This you know," said Hu, "but what about self-sacrifice? You need only be *willing* to skip ahead on the Tao." He stood and turned to the rear wall and plucked a pin from a square of *xuanzhi* paper and lifted it from its place among several others. Tân recognized his name inked on the rice-paper square.

Hu lowered the square along the Tao path and pushed the pin back into the wall.

Tân felt his eyes burn with embarrassment. He stared at the hundreds of squares on the wall, names of his family, his neighbors. He listened to the river play on the rocks beneath the floor of the temple but refused to be soothed. Tân longed to tear his name from the wall, all the names, and dump them in the river as it rushed away down the hill. Biting back the angry words inside him, he bowed and said, "Honorable sir, I do not understand."

"You have not learned from your experience," Hu said.

"But I have paid," Tân said. "My daughters have paid."

"Indeed," Hu said, lifting the rice-paper squares with his daughters' names painted on them, and replacing them fractionally higher than Tân's. "We're certain that your daughters have learned from their experience," Hu said.

He could not be calm. Before he embarrassed himself, Tân bowed—a chicken-like bob of his head, once to each priest, and turned to leave.

"Wait," Sheng said. "Did you not come for more souls?"

Tân wished to deny it and storm from the temple, but without the souls he cold not plow as much land. Without the land he could not buy his way to the next plateau on the path.

"Young souls," he demanded, knowing their eagerness to work would provide his plow with more power.

Hu held out a clay jar stoppered on both the top and the bottom with cork, and named a sum three times what Tân had paid the last time.

"Robbery," Tân said. "I won't pay that."

"Is any price too expensive to buy yourself a higher plane of existence?" asked Sheng.

Tân bowed. "I'd planned to donate two-thirds of what you ask for myself and my family's existential journey."

"Good deeds are worth more," Li said, raising the face of Chun Kwan to mask her own.

"And take much longer, honorable one," Tân said. He did not remind Li that Chun Kwan did not perform his good deeds until *after* he ascended into the heavens. Instead, Tân drew a wallet from the bag tied at his waist and handed over payment for the jar.

"We will gladly give over these souls for nothing," said Li, now wearing the smiling mask of the trickster Wu Zhen.

"If?" he asked.

"If you search your heart," said first-priest Sheng, slipping on the well-worn mask of Old Grandfather, "you'll know the answer and will place yourself firmly on the path."

Tân bowed and walked down the steps, then turned his back to the priests, retrieved his clogs, and made his way homeward, the sound of the wooden soles of his shoes striking off rocks and echoing on the stony path all the way down the hill.

Tân returned to his fields, stopping first at the small barn for a clay pot of resin from the mawei tree, and walked to the soul engine. He placed the jar of souls bottom-side-down over the mouth of the soul tank, and pulled the cork from the top of the jar.

There was little chance the souls would escape, as cold and thick as they were, but the double-cork mechanism helped to prevent their loss nonetheless. A string connecting the top cork to the bottom assured that both were plucked from the jar simultaneously. After Tan breached the jar, the enclosed souls flowed at a sluggish pace into the tank, plopping softly onto the bottom. Quickly, Tân removed the jar and capped the tank, sealing it with resin, before the souls realized freedom awaited but a handsbreadth above them.

He turned the crank to stir the souls and lit the pilot light to generate the small bit of heat to get the souls moving. The engine chugged to life and Tân said the prayer to the gods asking that these souls earn their higher rank on their path to Tao when they were done with their job for him.

He patted the top of the machine like one would pat a workhorse, then loosed the brake and guided it up a furrow.

It may have been a trick of the light, but when he reached the end of the field and turned the plow to the next row, he thought he saw a figure dart among his tangerine trees. Tân tied off the brake, but left the engine running as he made his way into the grove.

Quiet usually reigned in the grove, the dense foliage of the evergreens insulating it from sounds outside. Tân's feet rustled the dried leaves beneath the trees, sounding over-loud in his ears, but the noise didn't mask the sound of the six figures climbing among his largest tangerine trees.

Two climbed in the top-most boughs, pulling out the ripest, juiciest fruits and tossing them down to the four on the ground. The others sat in the leaves, backs to Tân, pulling the loose skins from the orange-red fruit and devouring them, hands shoving the pulpy fruit into mouths and reaching for another before the first could even be swallowed.

"You there!" he yelled. "Thieves! Get out of my trees!"

The rustling stopped, and the two men in the trees jumped to the ground. Those seated, rose and turned to Tân. In the shade of the trees, Tân found it hard to distinguish the features of the thieves, and he took a step forward to confront them, then halted abruptly. He recognized his uncle among them, his father's brother, one of the tree climbers.

His heart thumped in his chest, and he could feel a fine sheen of sweat break out on his forehead. Uncle Lao Weng had died more than twenty years ago. Tân and Heng had been newly wed when he had fallen down the well and drowned.

Tân found his anger leave abruptly. His body shook. He thought he would have been less fearful when meeting the ghost of his own ancestor. Still, he bowed deeply. "Uncle, my apologies. You are, of course, welcome to my tangerines, as are your companions. Is there else you would like?"

He looked closely at the others, recognizing none. Like Uncle Lao Weng, their faces were colorless. Clothes, too, were the color of bleached bone. At a distance, they'd looked to be wearing white, but this close to them, he could tell the whiteness derived from their state.

Lao Weng bowed. "We'll gladly take your tangerines, Tân, and anything else you may have to offer. We're hungry," he said, eyeing the fruit. "Hungry like we've not eaten in decades."

Tân said, "But why would you hunger, Uncle, when the village always provides for the ghosts?"

Lao Weng smiled and raised a hand to Tân's shoulder, turning him to face toward home. "It's hard to visit on the holy days when one is trapped in a reincarnation engine, nephew," he said, patting Tân across his shoulders with a hand that felt suspiciously solid for that of a ghost . . . solid, yet, soft and . . . *gummy,* as though it lacked bones, and perhaps skin, but held substance, nonetheless.

The reincarnated souls sat at his table, crowded together shoulder to shoulder, eating sticky rice balls, a bit of fish and more tangerines.

Heng scurried from table to stove, unsmiling, filling bowls, splashing water into cups, and hovering nearby, frowning at the mess they made of her house.

In the light, the ghosts were harder to see, a paleness against the luminance of day. In the place where they might once have had a belly hovered the consumed food they slurped and gobbled, a dark mass against the paleness. But they had no flesh to keep it in.

When Lao Weng reached for his third tangerine at the table, the action of bending at the waist extruded a glop of the masticated repast onto the dirt floor of the home. As if they didn't notice, the visitors continued to eat.

Tân looked at Heng with raised eyebrows. She shrugged back, the most minimal raise of shoulders as if not to draw attention to herself. Tân cleared his throat. "Uncle," he said, "I am honored to serve you in this life, but I am curious. . . ?"

Lao Weng looked up from his plate, smiling. "I know what you want to know," he said, reaching for another tangerine and turning back to the meal at hand. Between bites he said, "I didn't know when I gave my soul up to the reincarnation engine that the possibility even existed for me to return to this earth as *me*." He reached for a cup of water, lifted it quickly to his mouth, drank, and sat it back down again. "I am not the ghost of your ancestor, Tân, I *am* your ancestor, back to life, reincarnated in the engine, rather than the Tao."

Heng backed away from the table. Tân felt himself longing to do so as well. Not the ghost of his ancestor? But not really his ancestor. Then what? And how long did Uncle Lao Weng intend to stay?

Tân crossed the wooden bridge to the temple and rang the bamboo chime to request an audience with the priests. His face and hands felt the cold of the day, but he was warm from the hike. Only a moment passed before the rice-paper door slid open a fraction to admit him. Heat rolled out the door, warming his face.

Tân bowed. "I need an exorcism," he said.

Hu stepped back to admit Tân, then closed the door behind him.

"Perhaps you would like to pray first?" Hu said. He reached for a mask.

"To whom?" Tân asked.

"To the ancestor you wish to exorcise?"

"I have no need to pray to him when he is in my home, consuming my profits, as easy to converse with as you."

The recitation did not seem to phase Hu. Had he seen this before, Tân wondered?

Hu bowed, sliding the mask to a small table. He turned away from Tân and lit some incense in a small brazier, then bowed over it. "Let's talk of this exorcism," he said.

As head priest, Sheng performed the exorcism. She carried a mirror, etched with the eight spiritual trigrams around the edge, the symbols for sky, earth, water, fire, thunder, wind, mountain and lake, and led the way to Tân's house.

Hu carried a chicken and the ceremonial knife with which to slit its breast. Li brandished a staff with eight cross-arms at the top, each holding eight brass bells engraved with the eight trigrams. Tân pulled a cart containing six earthenware jars, one for each spirit invading his home.

The priests approached Tân's house, ringing the bells, flashing the mirror and chanting the exorcism ritual.

Lao Weng stood on the raised wooden porch as they arrived and said, "An exorcism! What ghosts do we banish today?" He smiled open-mouthed and Tân could count the wood grains on the weathered door of his house through Lao Weng's gaping maw. He felt the gorge rise up his throat, but forced it down. He could be brave with the priests here to help.

"Lao Weng." Sheng bowed. "We come to remove you and your friends. Would you be so kind as to enter the jar yourself?"

Tân removed the first jar from the cart and set it on the spot Sheng indicated.

Lao Weng laughed. "You cannot exorcise me," he said. "I am not a spirit." He walked down the steps holding a hand out to Sheng. "Feel me. Trust what your hands touch if you can't believe what your eyes see."

Sheng swung her hand in an arc as though she thought it would pass through Lao Weng's. It slapped against his, pushing it away.

He smiled. "See? Flesh. I am alive."

"Not quite," said Sheng, looking down at her palm, rubbing her thumb across the pads of her fingers, "but neither are you a ghost. You are . . . in between."

She turned to Tân. "Pack up the jars."

"But the exorcism?" Tân asked.

"We can't help with unwanted guests," Sheng said.

A strangled cry from the porch had them all turning to Heng. She rushed forward, *click, click, click,* and struck one of the half-reincarnated spirits in the back.

He flew off the porch, landing in the dirt by Sheng's feet. His flesh ripped, leaving a slit large enough for the soul to escape. A whining keen erupted from the tear.

Sheng reached for her mirror and motioned for Tân to open the nearest jar.

Vapor, like steam from a kettle, hissed from the reincarnated corpse. Sheng held the mirror above it, and with expertise learned from years of practice, rebounded the escaping soul into the jar.

Tân slammed down the lid.

Chanting, Li rang bells over the jar. Hu wrung the neck of the chicken and gutted it, then marked the jar with blood. Sheng dropped the mirror and with intricate hand motions, performed the *mudra* necessary to seal the soul within.

Heng stared in open-mouthed horror from the porch, but quickly snapped from her stupor. She rushed forward again and shoved the four remaining souls from the porch. Four more times, Sheng used the mirror to direct souls into earthenware jars.

Lao Weng said to Sheng. "You condone this?"

Sheng bowed. "I can neither condone nor not condone."

"But this is murder!" Lao Weng said.

"I'm not so sure," said Sheng, "since you are neither alive nor dead. I will meditate upon it." She turned to leave. "By custom, you are still welcome in Tân's home."

"And be murdered in my sleep?"

"Sleep?" interjected Tân, "You have not slept yet! All you do is eat, eat, eat."

"He is not welcome at your hearth?" Sheng asked, turning to Tân and lifting a brow.

Tân looked to Heng. With a negative shake, perhaps imperceptible to the others, she let Tân know her wishes. He would serve a special penance in the bureaucracy of hell for that, he knew, but he was willing. Heng gave him the courage.

"No," Tân said. "He is not welcome."

Sheng said to Lao Weng. "You may stay with us."

Tân's face burned with shame. What he was not willing to do, the priests would do in his place. He would have to increase his temple donations twice-over for them to keep up with Lao Weng's appetite.

Sheng said, "Load the jars back on the cart. Lao Weng—" she turned to him, raising her left arm in a gesture of fellowship, "join me, please. We will walk together."

"It is a trick!" Lao Weng said, stumbling backward and rushing headlong up the stairs toward Heng.

Fear covered Heng's face. She ran to the door of the house.

Lao Weng hurdled up the remaining steps and *leapt* into Heng's body.

His pale, boneless self sank beneath Heng's tanned flesh and disappeared.

Heng screamed and ran back and forth on the porch, jumping and flailing as Lao Weng sought control of her body.

Tân knew the instant his Uncle won: Heng quieted, and the peaceful light in her eyes turned to triumph. The voice was Heng's but the words were Lao Weng's: "See what comes of denying your ancestor his due, Tân?" Lao Weng laughed, Heng's eyes squeezed closed like Tân remembered his uncle's used to do.

When they were little, he and his cousins had called the laughing Lao Weng *piggy*, with his squinting eyes and big cheeks. And a pig is what he had become, in death, if not in life. Tân's hand itched to slap the satisfied look from Lao Weng's face. How shameful, that his Uncle desired life so much that he would steal someone else's.

Anger seared his chest.

"Can you do nothing, now?" Tân asked Sheng. "Surely Heng is not dead?" Tân felt his heart catch. Tears scalded his eyes. He had not thought of that possibility until just now.

"She's not dead," said Sheng, and Tân felt himself relax. "Lao Weng has pushed her aside and taken over her body."

"But you can remove him," Tân said.

Sheng nodded. "I can."

"Then do so!"

"This is an unusual exorcism," Sheng said. "The astrology must be exactly right. We must take care not to harm Heng's soul."

"Hurry," said Tân. "While we discuss it, Heng must abide that pig inside her skin."

Sheng bent to knock a bit of dust from the hem of her robe. "I must think," she said.

"I'll pay," Tân said. "Whatever you want, I'll pay. Now help her." He looked at Heng and saw only Lao Weng. He turned away, unable to bear the sight of him.

"Whatever *I* want?" Sheng said. "I want nothing."

"What will it take?" said Tân.

Sheng said, "You have two choices: Heng or no Heng. What would you pay to have Heng?"

Tân sank to his knees moaning, his hand pressed against his ears, his eyes tightly shut. "I'll do it," he said, dropping his hands and looking up. "I pledge my soul to the engines." His voice became flat. "Now please save Heng."

Sheng said, "Only your willingness is required. You may yet have your wish and avoid the engines." She nodded at Hu.

Hu tightened his grasp on the ceremonial knife. He sped to Heng, vaulting onto the porch, and sank the blade hilt-deep into her right shoulder.

Tân looked on with horror, the event happening so quickly, he couldn't voice his denial. Heng staggered, the wooden treads of her shoes thudding unevenly on the porch as she appeared to search for balance. Her face paled, and she sank back against the wall of the house, supported by Hu.

The edges of her figure blurred and Lao Weng pitched forward, peeled from her body. He somersaulted off the porch, landing in the dirt on his back. At his right shoulder, a hole gaped in the whiteness of his flesh. No blood poured forth.

As if unwilling to shed the skin it so recently wore, Lao Weng's soul took long moments to exit the wound. Only slender, tentative curls of vapor exited the slash. Sheng lifted the bells at her waist in one hand and her mirror in the other. Baiting the soul, she shook the bells in an intricate pattern, their brass intonations dull in the humid afternoon.

Like a moth to flame, Lao Weng's soul swooped through the hole and battered into Sheng's mirror.

Tân waited, lid poised open over the last empty jar.

Lao Weng's soul caromed off the underside and slid helpless into the earthenware container. Tân slammed down the lid, then sank to his knees breathing deeply. He looked up at Sheng.

"I don't understand," he said. "You said you could do naught. Then there was talk of murder, and yet," he broke off and turned to Hu, pointing. "You came forward and . . . as if you had planned the taking of his soul."

Hu smiled, and Sheng looked as though she might like to. *Pity,* Tân thought, *they couldn't hide behind their masks here.*

Sheng said, "We had no plan other than exorcism when we came today," she said. "Opportunity presented itself when Lao Weng stole Heng's body. Hu knew exactly what to do. And so, your problem is solved. With your help, we shall return these souls to the temple so that they might be cleansed. Would you be interested in using them again?" she asked.

Tân shook his head. "No."

"But these souls have worked for you for years," she said. "They know what to expect of you, you know what to expect of them."

"I know more about these souls than I care to know."

Sheng nodded, then turned to Hu and Li who had begin the ritual binding of the corpses on shrouds of white. Tân could see that neither looked happy. He knew corpse binding provided little joy for anyone, but this task irritated more than most. As Li and Hu grasped the bodies by shoulder and ankle, the bodies ripped as easily as the flesh of the tangerines growing in the fields beyond his house.

He turned away. Heng bloodied and bandaged, watched tight-lipped from the porch. She would not leave, he knew, until all the bodies were gone.

Nonetheless, his heart felt light, as he loaded the jars onto the cart and began the journey back to the temple. He might eventually spend time in an engine, perhaps in one of these very jars, but the rest of his family would not.

He smiled. Good deeds cost nothing, but were more valuable than a lifetime of profits.

~

Kelly A. Harmon *used to write truthful, honest stories about authors and thespians, senators and statesmen, movie stars and murderers. Now she writes lies, which is infinitely more satisfying, but lacks the convenience of doorstep delivery, especially on rainy days . . . which is to say: Ms. Harmon is a former magazine and newspaper reporter and* editor. Her recent publication credits include articles at the SciFi Channel's on-line magazine, SciFi Weekly *and short fiction published in* Black Dragon, White Dragon, *a Ricasso Press anthology. Her award-winning novella,* "Blood Soup", *is slated for publication by Eternal Press in September. Read more about Ms. Harmon at her Website, www.kellyaharmon.com.*

Broken Things

Kathryn Board

Ellen fell on her mother's couch, so exhausted that her head hurt. She hadn't been home in over five years—not even for Christmas—and she didn't want to be here now. *Who, besides my mother, dies in her sleep at age sixty-five?* She had asked herself the same question for days. It just didn't make any sense; not even the coroner could offer an explanation. She remembered his sympathetic expression when she arrived at the morgue to identify her mother's body. He suspected suicide. Ellen's mother was diagnosed with pancreatic cancer only six weeks before and she had already complained to her doctors about the pain. But, no. The toxicology came back clean and the cause of death was listed as "multiple organ failure." Whatever killed her mother, it had probably spared her months, if not years, of suffering.

Ellen poured herself a glass of wine and opened a package of cookies. Comfort food—because as unwilling as Ellen had been to visit her clingy, demanding mother, her death left Ellen with crippling guilt and unexpected loneliness. Ellen took a long drink of the Chablis. She wanted to get drunk and forget about funerals, probate, and death in general. She put her head back and closed her dry eyes.

That is, until a voice—an *accusation*—splintered the silence.

"You broke my bottle!"

Ellen jumped to her feet and dropped her glass, spilling her wine. Without thinking, she grabbed the first weapon she saw: a knitting needle from her mother's knitting basket. She gripped it like a knife in front of her.

"Who's there?"

No response. She scanned the small room. Clearly, she was alone. But she *knew* she had heard a voice.

"Who's there?" she demanded.

No answer. Nobody in sight. But a breath of warm air, like an eddy from something in motion, stirred her hair.

Ellen didn't lower the knitting needle. "Mom?" she whispered.

"No." The voice was deep, resonating, and definitely male. It came from right in front of her. "Your mother is dead. I have no mistress. I have no bottle. I am nothing."

The voice had a dull, colorless tone that spoke of anguish beyond solace. Ellen felt a flash of irritation. Even disembodied voices mourned her mother more than she did. Her temper flared and she snapped at the empty room. "Look, I don't know what you want or how you know my mother but—"

"I was your mother's servant. Her al-jinn. Her jinni. Her genie."

Genie. The word froze Ellen's anger and she sank back down on the couch. Impossible. Genies didn't exist. There just *couldn't* be an invisible one in her mom's living room. She looked at the wine glass that still lay on the carpet. She wished that she were drunk and could dismiss this nonsense as a hallucination. But she hadn't even finished her first glass.

"You're a genie," Ellen said, disbelief shading her tone. "You mean, *literally* a genie. You grant wishes."

"I did. I was your mother's for the last thirty-five years and now I should be yours. But without my bottle, I am invisible, incorporeal . . . useless. For hours, you couldn't even hear me."

Another breath of warm air. Ellen didn't know where to look when she spoke. "You said that I broke your bottle."

"Yes."

"Can you tell me where it is?"

The swirling breath of air was warm against her cheek and the voice was right in front of her. "Your mother's bedroom. You broke it and you packed it in a box."

She got up and went into her mother's bedroom. There had to be three dozen boxes stacked into two unsteady towers against the wall. One stack for storage and the other to ship back home to Philly. "I'm going to need some help," Ellen said.

"Third from the top," the genie replied. "The stack on the left."

Ellen shifted the boxes until she got to the one she wanted and ripped off the packing tape. Photo albums. A couple of her mother's old purses. And a wooden box. Ellen remembered packing it. It had fallen off of a shelf in the closet and slammed against her shoulder before hitting the floor. She had a pretty nasty bruise. Ellen had practically thrown the box into the packing crate.

Ellen ran her hand over the intricate etching, opened the latch, and lifted the lid. There it was. The bottle. It had only broken into three pieces: the fat body cleaved in two and the slender mouth snapped off at the neck. The glass was smoky-gray with an opalescent shimmer and of a sturdy thickness.

"My bottle," the genie said from over her shoulder. He sounded heartbroken.

Ellen picked up one of the pieces of glass. "Why didn't Mom tell me about you?" she asked.

"She tried to call you." There was a reprimand in the voice. "She wanted to tell you before she died."

"She called a hundred times a day and never mentioned it. I talked to her at least four times last week alone."

"She was lonely for you. She wanted you to come home so she could tell you in person."

The genie's words reminded Ellen of the six unanswered voicemails on her cell phone from her mother on the evening before she died. The guilt nauseated her. Ellen clenched her jaw. "Bullshit. You said that you were with her for thirty-five years. She had plenty of one-on-one time to reveal the fact that she had a genie in the closet." She toyed with the broken bottle pieces. "None of this makes any sense. Why didn't she just wish for you to cure her?"

The breath of air fluttered the curtains, then the box flap, and finally, Ellen's hair, as if the genie was pacing the room in agitation. "I begged her to let me make her well but she wouldn't. It would have been her third wish. I would have had to return to my bottle. Like I told you, she was lonely and in pain. She didn't want to be alone and she didn't want to be a burden. She said it was her time."

Ellen gave a dry, harsh laugh. "Yeah, right. She was fine with criticizing me and nagging me and questioning my judgment but asking for help might burden me." Ellen took a deep breath. "Do you have a name?"

"Vimm."

"Look, Vimm, it's probably better if we don't talk about my mother." She took a couple more deep breaths. "I am sorry I broke your bottle, though. What happens to you now?"

His voice was right beside her. "I cannot grant wishes. I have no mistress. In three sunsets, I will become mortal, like you."

She could hear his distress, his fear. *I was your mother's servant. Her al-jinn. Her jinni. Her genie.* Ellen sighed, knowing what her mother would expect her to do. Besides, she wasn't looking forward to finishing sorting her mother's things and she wasn't in any hurry to get back to her empty apartment in Philly. Maybe, if she could make things right, she would get three wishes in the bargain. Ellen knew just what her first wish would be. . . .

Three sunsets. Vimm would be mortal by sunset on Thursday. It wasn't very long at all. She took another steadying breath. "How can I help?" she asked.

Ellen wanted to kick her mother's computer. It was close to eight years old, connected to the internet via dial-up, and making some strange noises. Her mother had only used it for e-mail and even that must have taken considerable patience. Right now, patience was something Ellen had very little of. She needed some quick answers on how to blow or repair glass.

If she wanted to save Vimm, she had a little more than two and a half days left to repair the bottle or make him a new one. *Make* him one, not *buy* him one. Vimm had explained very carefully that whoever crafted or fixed his bottle was his next master. She could repair the glass she had broken or she could make him something new, but she couldn't purchase a bottle that someone else had made. Vimm had sounded *extremely* agitated at the idea of belonging to anyone else. Ellen's best idea was to find a glass blower who could advise her. She would have given good money to know where her mother's Yellow Pages were. The computer was so slow that she couldn't view video and half of the pictures wouldn't load.

Ellen gritted her teeth. "God, I with this thing was faster."

"Don't."

Ellen looked up at the empty room. "Don't what?"

"Wish," Vimm said. "It hurts that I can't grant it."

"Sorry." Ellen tapped her foot and looked at the monitor. She might have found the website for a local glass-blower. "I'm just saying that there are people who do professional glass repair. If this computer worked a little faster, I'd already be talking to one."

"You must be the one to fix my bottle, Ellen—"

"I know. Jesus. Stop nagging. I'm not going to let someone else fix your bottle. I just need advice."

"I would rather be mortal than belong to some other family," Vimm reminded her.

Ellen snorted in frustration. "I'm not going to give you to someone else. Would you please trust me? You're as bad as my mother."

"That's funny," Vimm said. "You remind me very much of her, too."

"I am *not* like her. She was negative and stubborn and pushy. . . ."

Vimm's voice sounded stern. "Perhaps, but she was also kind and loyal and nurturing. I see those qualities in you. It would be an honor to learn how to be mortal from you."

For the first time since the funeral, Ellen felt her throat tighten. She struggled against her tears. She had barely slept; she was frustrated; and she was faced with the possibility that Vimm had seen a side of her mother that she had never known. "You don't want to learn from me," she said in a choked voice. "I have this little apartment in Philly and spend half of my time reading. I hardly have any friends; I don't have a pet. Hell, I can't even keep *plants* alive, Vimm. I'm not the person to teach you how to be mortal."

They were both silent for a few moments. "There!" Ellen said as the webpage finished loading. "Finally." She grabbed her cell phone and dialed.

A bored-sounding woman answered the phone. "Morning. Morton's Glass Repair."

"Hi. I have a piece of broken glass—"

"You're going to need to bring it in," the woman interrupted. "We can't give estimates until we see what type of glass it is and how bad the damage is."

Ellen took a deep breath. "No. I need to repair it myself. I was calling for advice."

Now, the woman sounded bored and annoyed. "You want to fix the glass yourself?"

"Yes," said Ellen.

"And you want my advice?"

"Yes."

"Don't use Super Glue," the woman said. "When your home repairs don't work, you'll really piss off a professional if he has to chunk Super Glue off of your glass. Good b—"

"Wait. You do glassblowing there, right?" Ellen asked.

Annoyance was edging out boredom in the woman's voice. "Yes, we do."

"What if I wanted to blow a glass bottle? If I was willing to pay for a private lesson, could someone there teach me how to do it?"

Ellen actually heard the woman sigh. "I'm sorry, but for insurance reasons, we can't let customers use the furnace."

"But I'd sign a waiver and pay—"

"Look lady," the woman said loudly, "we have a variety of ready-made pieces that you could buy. We can probably repair your glass if you bring it in. But if you want to make something yourself, I suggest you join a pottery class." There was a faint click and the line went silent.

Vimm's voice was right beside Ellen. "Did she help?" he asked.

Ellen thought about it for a moment. "You know, I think she did."

"I'm back," Ellen called, letting herself in the front door of her mother's house. "Vimm?"

She looked around the living room and saw the curtain flutter. "I'm here," Vimm said. "How did it go?"

"The woman who teaches the pottery class thinks I'm nuts," Ellen replied, walking into the kitchen and laying her purse on the counter. "She couldn't figure out why I insisted on making a bottle. She kept trying to get me to make a bowl."

"It's easier," Vimm replied.

"No doubt." Ellen turned on the gas burner under the tea kettle. "I hope you don't care if your new home is lopsided, lumpy, and looks more like a stick-shift than a bottle."

Ellen thought she heard Vimm chuckle. "I don't."

"Good," Ellen said, getting a teabag. "It has to dry for two days and then they're going to fire it Thursday afternoon. It's cutting it close, I know, but we'll have it back in time."

"Thank you so much, Ellen."

"Don't thank me yet," Ellen said. "We don't even know if pottery can hold you. It may *have* to be glass."

Vimm's motions made the gas flame sputter under the kettle. "I don't know," he said. "It's the only bottle I've ever had. It was fashioned by a master glassblower. I was a wedding gift for his daughter. It was his most sturdy piece."

Ellen spooned sugar into her cup. "I was thinking that we should try to repair your bottle in case the pottery thing doesn't work."

"How?" Vimm asked.

Ellen looked at the flame under the kettle and wondered how hot it was. "I have a few ideas. . . ."

Ellen leaned over her mother's gas stove, the flame turned all the way up on the front burner. In one hand, she grasped the neck of the broken bottle with a pair of barbeque tongs, holding the jagged edge in the flame. In the other, she held half of the body of the bottle in an oven mitt.

Theoretically, it should work. Glass *did* melt at *some* temperature. The woman from the glass repair place had mentioned a furnace. Clearly, the stove was nowhere near that hot but Ellen hoped that it didn't need to be to melt the thin, broken edges and meld the pieces back together. So far, she hadn't had any luck.

"It isn't melting," Ellen said.

"Give it a little longer," Vimm advised. "It was very sturdy glass."

Ellen inspected the edge of the bottle neck and put it back into the flame. It was already nearly sunset on Tuesday and Ellen felt like time was pressing down on them. She had been thinking about the genie's good opinion of her mother. She was torn between clinging to her resentment and asking him questions. She took a deep breath and worked to keep her voice calm. "Vimm . . . would you tell me something about my mother?"

"What do you want to know?" he asked.

"Anything," she replied softly, staring at the piece of glass in the flame. "I think you might have known her better than I did."

Vimm was quiet for a moment, and then said, "She was in a movie once."

"Really? Which one?"

"I don't know. It was a zombie movie."

Ellen felt a little floored. "No shit."

"They were filming near her home, she said, and needed extras." Vimm paused. "She told me that it was the most fun she ever had, covered in chocolate syrup, shambling around with a bunch of other extras. . . ."

Ellen tried to imagine it. She thought about her mother—her somber, stodgy mother—dressed as a zombie, and she made a sound that was somewhere between a laugh and a sob. Laughter won out. She couldn't stop. Before she knew it, tears streaked her face and her stomach hurt. She had to lay down the bottle pieces so that she wouldn't drop them. When she had gathered herself, she said, "Thanks, Vimm. That was exactly what I needed."

Ellen squinted at the edge of the glass. It looked every bit as sharp as it had when she had started. "The stove isn't going to melt it," she said. "We're going to have to try something else." She turned off the burner.

"Something hotter?" Vimm asked.

Ellen tried to think. "A propane torch, maybe?" She had a mental image of herself setting her mother's house on fire. "I just don't know anything about working with glass," Ellen said. "Maybe we need a whole new strategy."

"Like what?" Vimm asked. Ellen looked to where she heard the genie's voice and saw a faint shimmer. There was a wavering in the air, like heat convections or a mirage.

"I think I can almost see you," Ellen said softly.

The mirage wavered again. "I am closer to being mortal."

"Then I'd better get going." Ellen laid the bottle pieces on the kitchen counter top and grabbed the keys to her mom's old truck. "Stay here," she told him.

There was an arts and crafts store at the mall. Surely, they must have *something* that bonded to glass. Something besides Super Glue. They only had two days left before Vimm became mortal. Whatever she was going to try, she needed to do it *fast*.

Vimm became fully visible, with well-defined edges, only about three hours before sunset on Thursday. His hair was orange and gold flames. His skin was stark black and he towered over Ellen at nearly seven feet. For the first half hour, she had a hard time not staring at him.

There were two bottles on the kitchen counter: her off-kilter, clay-colored pottery creation that she had just retrieved from the ceramics class and the glass bottle, glued together and scarred with cracks. The glue that she had bought claimed to harden in one to three days. They had waited as long as they could, but, according to the local weather, the sun would set in another ten minutes.

"So, how do we know if it worked?" Ellen asked.

"I will . . . try it," Vimm said, looking the glass bottle. "You should stand back."

She edged to the doorway between the kitchen and the living room. Vimm's body seemed to dissolve, to sublimate into a sooty smoke. It poured into the glass bottle in a steady stream. Ellen watched. She couldn't blink. Vimm's smoke continued to flow into it, and the bottle shivered and vibrated.

"Be careful, Vimm," Ellen said.

Without pausing, all of the smoke found its way into the repaired bottle. For a moment, Ellen thought that it might work. But, then, cracks formed over the surface. Black smoke leaked through the fissures and the bottle made a splintering sound. Ellen ducked around the corner and heard the glass bottle explode. When she peeked into the kitchen, Vimm stood there looking at the destruction all around him—pieces of glass *and* pottery. The force of the explosion had knocked the pottery bottle off of the counter and it had shattered on the floor.

"Shit!" Ellen said, looking at the mess helplessly. She glanced at the clock. Sunset was in five minutes. There wasn't time for anything else. Ellen could tell from Vimm's expression that he had come to the same conclusion.

"It's not bad . . . being mortal," Ellen said, trying to sound optimistic.

Vimm shook his head. "You mortals want a lot of things."

"I don't," Ellen replied. "If we had been able to fix your bottle, I only would have needed one wish."

"Tell me."

"I would have wished to not be alone," Ellen replied, thinking of her little, empty apartment in Philly.

Vimm smiled a little. "I want to tell you something else about your mother. You are so like her. I want you to know what *she* wished for."

Ellen opened her mouth and closed it. Did she really want to know? Ellen glanced at the clock. Three minutes. "OK."

"She wished for a painless death," Vimm said.

Suddenly, her mother's frantic calls on the night of her death and the coroner's vague report made sense. Ellen felt her eyes tear up and swallowed against the lump in her throat. "And you gave her one."

Vimm smile grew sad. "Yes."

"What else?"

"To always have enough to meet her needs," Vimm answered. Ellen thought about growing up and going to college. They had never been rich, but it wasn't until she moved out that she'd ever worried about money.

"There's three wishes, right?" Ellen asked.

"Thirty-five years ago, she made her first wish." He stepped closer to Ellen. "The very first thing she wished for, was you."

"No. . . !" Ellen said, almost numb. "Really?"

Vimm nodded. "She was infertile, unmarried, and wanted a child. I gave her you."

Ellen's head swam. Her mother had wished for her. The clinginess suddenly made sense. Aside from Vimm, she had been the only person that her mother had ever had.

Vimm closed his eyes. "It's time," he said. "Thank you for all you tried to do." And then, he leaned into Ellen, his face very close to hers, like he was going to kiss her.

Ellen pulled back, surprised. "What the hell are you doing?"

The genie didn't answer. Instead he dissolved into black smoke. The smoke poured between her lips, down her throat, into her belly. It gave her a hot flush, like she had just swallowed a shot of whiskey too fast. The last of the smoke disappeared just as the last ray of sun faded from the kitchen window. Ellen felt a flutter within her. She ran her hand over her torso and felt a slight swell at her stomach.

Oh my God. "Vimm, you sonofabitch," she said aloud, her voice shaking, "my *mother* asked for a child, not me!" She felt a wave of nausea and sank into one of the kitchen chairs.

ShitShitShitShit. She couldn't raise a child. She just *couldn't.* For a moment, for the briefest moment, she considered an abortion. She didn't have to go through with this. After the way Vimm had violated her. . . .

Ellen's own words echoed in her head: *I would have wished to not be alone.* This must have been Vimm's best attempt to grant her one and only wish. She sighed and ran her hand over the swell of her torso again.

"This is a bad idea, Vimm," she said. "I told you—I *kill plants.*" She felt movement in her, like bubbles, as if Vimm was trying to answer her. "Oh, weird," she whispered.

Ellen pressed her cold hands to her face. But even through her fear, she knew that she couldn't abandon Vimm. He didn't want to belong to anyone else and she didn't want to be alone. If she saw this pregnancy through, she could make both of their wishes come true. She lifted her shirt and looked at the tiny, unfamiliar rise of her stomach. "Want to see what's on TV?" she asked. "I'm in the mood for a bad zombie movie."

~

Kathryn Board earned an undergraduate degree in English and Biology and went on to earn her M.A. in immunology. Currently, she works in a medical research lab at the University of Pittsburgh. She has had published several short works of non-fiction, but this is her first credit as a fiction author.

Audition for Evil

Amy Treadwell

Charla Malignissima Esmerelda di Malfeasance scowled at her blackened Mirror. Mischievous faces twittered from oak leaves and curls carved in the frame, but the Mirror's surface absorbed her infamous baron-withering stare with nonchalance. She tried stalking six paces across the chamber and then flinging the glare over her shoulder with a swirl of robes and flickering candles. Nothing.

Her eyebrow broke its slow, calculated rise with a twitch.

A contralto drawled from the corner, "If a sorceress pouts in non-reflective magic mirror, is she still over-acting?"

Charla twitched her robes. She wasted another exquisite stare on the Mirror. "Those who live above cook-pots shouldn't throw stones."

The Chancellor ruffled his feathers and hopped from his gilded cage to a nearer perch.

"Eat me, and you'll end up navigating this labyrinth of rites and rituals without even a Mirror." He jabbed his beak for emphasis and cocked his head to study her through his monocle. "You'd have to crawl back to the HAG and request to audition in person. No filmy overlays. No sourceless radiance dial. An unfiltered audition." He blinked a magnified eye, a bright sheen of vengeful glee caught by the candelabras. "Your illusion of youth and beauty will vanish like a soap bubble."

Charla's stage presence gave her a painful twinge, but she buried it. She brushed jeweled fingers across the wand at her belt, and the bird sidled on his perch. "Then it is lucky that you are useful to me." She caught him and raised him to eye level. "The Mirror, Chancellor. Before I regret my decision to merely clip your wings."

She strode to the enchanted heirloom. It loomed, with a span broad enough to encompass her elaborate cascading tiered gown, the dark crepe and cobweb she reserved for christenings. The once-lively surface hung dead as a fish-eye. She tossed the bird at the Mirror, startling him into helpless flapping. A few feathers drifted down as he resettled on an outcropping of the frame with a glare.

"Well?"

"I'm thinking!" He nipped at her irritably.

"Think out loud." She left the Chancellor prodding at an outcropping of curls and paced around the Mirror, wand idly tapping against her lips.

The Hexagonal Alliance for Glamourie were a cloistered, moldering clique of unmitigated snobs, which made her yearn all the more to join. Membership requirements included sixteen specified iniquitous acts, uninterrupted observation of the arcane rites for 12 cycles of the astrological calendar, the collection of no less than six hundred and forty-four rare herbs and spell enhancements, induction into the Enchantresses of Distinction milli-quarterly, and lastly, an audition in which the candidate must demonstrate guile, wit, charm, and instinctive wickedness.

Eons of practice before the Mirror had honed her presentation. Her guile and wit were unsurpassed; these last many centuries, she had bound her most contentious advisor in avian form, thus capturing for herself an unrivaled sparring partner who, though not quite her equal, kept her mind and tongue admirably sharp. And charm was mostly presence, hauteur, if you will. Age had not been kind to her, true, but perhaps she could make that up through extra wickedness.

Then again, her instinct for wickedness was somewhat erratic. . . .

Charla flicked a longing glance toward the Mirror. The HAG allowed each candidate only one audition per life. If she failed, death of shame followed by reincarnation would be her only avenue into the hallowed hexagon of the HAG. And half the time, sorceresses reincarnated as imbecilic woodland animals, like bunnies. She shuddered. Without the Mirror, even her formidable glare and acidic wit might not be enough to counter her disadvantage in evil.

The Chancellor hopped from curl to leaf, scratching at the carvings and muttering under his breath. "Have you practiced regularly scheduled maintenance?"

Charla paused with wand to lips. "I distinctly remember spritzing it with a vial of unicorn tears not half a century ago."

"And the frame?"

"Rubbed with spider venom twice monthly." She waved her wand. "You've seen the gnome come by."

The Chancellor peered into the dull surface. "I don't trust gnomes. They tell you it's genuine spider venom, but do you ever see a bandaged hand?" He laid a claw on the Mirror's surface and scritched.

The sorceress squinted at the bird perched a stepladder's height above her head. "Are you sure you know what you're doing? You're making it worse!"

The little bird ignored her and peered into the blackened Mirror for five heartbeats. He turned with uncharacteristic solemnity. "It's dead, Mistress."

The Chancellor resettled his monocle and tucked in his wings. "The animus, however weak, should have stirred at such deliberate disfigurement. It needs reanimation. A drop of heart's blood, gathered as Saturn's ascending, and we'll have it in working order. Let's check the astronomical calendar—oh, capital! That's tonight! Now all you need is a superfluous staff member; the gardener would work, or perhaps the milk maid, but it's a pity there's no one ready at hand. . . ."

A feather drifted to the floor.

The Chancellor tried very hard to blend into the woodwork.

Charla Malignissima Esmerelda di Malfeasance bore the inscrutable visage of a royal executioner. She laid her wand lightly against her lips.

"Instinctive wickedness. . . ."

The Chancellor made himself smaller. "The laundress is raising six children while caring for a dying father. She comes this Tuesday."

"I need blue blood, the higher-born the better. What was your grandsire's title?"

"Pig-keeper!"

"Baron of Higglesby, wasn't he? And your grandame a contessa?"

"I was born out of wedlock!"

Charla strode to her bookshelves in a swirl of robes. She knelt, extracted a leather volume, and patted it fondly. The bird watched from under one wing as she hauled it to her spell podium and threw it open.

"Baron Ivanesco von Higglesby and Contessa Vian—oh, her father was actually—that makes him a Marque. I hadn't realized your breeding was so refined."

The Chancellor shouted from behind the frame, "I have it on good authority the cook's boy is a prince in hiding!"

Charla narrowed her eyes. "A prince in hiding? Hmm." She paused. Instinctive wickedness tugged at her wizened heartstrings. "Killing you would be more wicked by far."

Silence greeted her. She tasted the space it made, considering. Without the Chancellor, these chambers would ring with her unquestioned perfidy. She could step into the gilded heights of the HAG with silence as her only companion.

Charla closed the book. "Perhaps the prince will do. That boy always had a docile temper. Come back down."

"I'll wait 'til Saturn is out of phase."

Charla paused. "Do you not trust me, Chancellor?"

"I'm more comfortable up here."

"If I made you my Mirror, you'd likely retain every drop of acid. Etched glass would spoil the effect."

"I reflect but truth. Consider, the etched lines might not come from the glass. ”

"Then come down."

"You are a sorceress, Madam."

A wry grin curled one side of her lips. The Chancellor didn't trust her.

She tapped the wand against her lips with a girlish smile. Instinctive wickedness might not be an obstacle after all.

A nervous feather drifted out from behind the frame.

"I think I've changed my mind about the live audition."

"Capital! Off you go."

She laughed, bouncing her cackle off the blackened Mirror and sending it careening around the chamber. A shower of feathers shivered down.

In the eyes of her sharpest critic, she had given an utterly convincing performance.

~

Amy Treadwell likes to write what she likes to read: characters that sound like real people. Her work has been published in the 2008 Triangulation anthology, Flash Fiction Online, and has won first and second prize in the 2008 PARSEC contest. She has taught writing classes for the University of Oklahoma, the Oklahoma Writing Project, and Moore High School. In her spare time, she enjoys kayaking, traveling, and reading fantasy. Her website is http://members.cox.net/amytreadwell.

One Touch to Remember

David Seigler

Dirty rain fell on Lancaster; gray matter droppings that muted the skyline and cast the world in a single hue. Jennifer weaved from awning to awning, dodging the vicious downpour before finding herself in front of an old, two-story brick building, recently renovated as part of the city's reclamation project.

It wasn't particularly inviting, Jennifer thought, which made her decision to go inside all the more curious. The door swung open just as she reached for it. An older woman, elegantly dressed and with a streak of gray in her hair rushed out, nearly knocking Jennifer to the ground in the process.

The woman stopped, giving Jennifer a look that was at once distraught, vacant, haunted, and confused. Then she straightened and hurried away, oblivious of the rain.

Once inside, Jennifer shook the rain from her thick hair and detangled the glass pendant that hung from her neck. The room was spacious, exposed ducts adding character to the high ceiling. It was filled throughout with wooden pedestals on which rested various metal sculptures; a few were small and delicate, but most were massive and ugly. At the back of the room a rotund man attempted to waddle his way down a set of precarious wooden stairs.

"And what would bring," he said between gulps of breath, "a girl like you out on such a foul day, hmmmm?"

"Oh! I'm . . . well, I'm job hunting, actually," she said.

The man gave a hearty laugh, which set his bulbous jowls to flapping. "There are no jobs to be had these days."

"I see," she said and began to look about the room.

After examining a few innocuous statues, she came across one that intrigued her. Two children sat in a boat which listed lazily to its side. She gazed at it for several moments before announcing, "I'd like to work here."

"No, I'm afraid not."

"Why not?" she persisted. "I'm a hard worker, really!"

"Ah, I'm sure you are," he said. "Alas, I'm but a humble artist. I've nothing left to pay someone such as you."

"But you wouldn't have to," Jennifer pushed. "I don't need money. My grandmother left me enough money to live on. It's just . . . well, my parents think it's important that I have something to do."

"Do they, now?" he laughed. "Well, I'm sorry, but I just don't have anything for you to do."

"I could clean!" she said. "I could watch the place when you have to be gone. Please."

She gave him her best lopsided smile. It usually worked.

"I'm sorry, no," he said.

Defeated, she returned to the metal sculpture. Fascinated, she reached out to touch it. It felt cold, wrong somehow.

"Then I'd like to buy this."

"Have an interest in art, do you?" he asked.

"Not usually," Jennifer replied. "It's just . . . my brother was killed on a boat. I don't know, this just . . . reminded me of him."

He stood for a moment, lost in thought. Then he finally said, "Alright, then. I might can find something for you to do. But just for a few hours a day, no weekends."

"You mean it?" Jennifer almost jumped. "You won't regret this, Mr. . . ."

The man let out a weary sigh.

"Well, if you're going to be working here, you should call me Roy."

"How's the new job going?" her mother asked without looking up from her catalog.

"It's okay. I mostly just clean." Jennifer poured a bowl of cereal and sat down.

"I don't know why you agreed to work without pay. It doesn't even sound like a real job."

"You just said I had to get a job, mother. You didn't say anything about it paying. You know what the economy's like. This will at least give me something for my resumé."

"Yes, but, surely you could find something better than this. Look, I know you can live off your grandmother's trust for awhile, but you still have to grow up. It's been two years since Jeff's accident. You can't mope forever."

"Funny how everything always comes back to Jeff." Jennifer swirled the cereal around in the bowl, no longer hungry.

"We don't blame you for what happened, honey. We just . . . we just want you to move on."

Jennifer got up from the table. This was a conversation she had memorized long ago.

Jennifer finished sweeping the wooden floor and turned to the task of dusting the metal sculptures. She paused at the figure of the two children in the boat. As before, she reached out to touch it just as Roy came up behind her.

"Tell me about your family," he said, startling her.

"There's not much to tell," she answered. "There's just my parents and me now that . . . now that my brother's gone."

The man looked at her intensely. "That must . . ." he said, with a touch of wariness. "That must be difficult."

Jennifer continued to stare at the sculpture. "It was an accident. He was doing drugs and . . . there was an accident." She was angry at herself for growing morose again. "It was two years ago. You'd think I'd be dealing with it a little better by now."

"So time is a healer, eh?" he said, brightening. "But who's to say the proper dose?"

Jennifer forced a smile.

"Well, then," he said. "What you need is something special to brighten your day. I've got just the thing." He waved his hand in a broad motion. "My sculpture work is merely trinkets to pay the bills, nothing more. Upstairs I have work that is much more . . . challenging."

He flashed an odd smile that revealed a row of tiny teeth. There was something predatory about the smile, Jennifer thought. It set off vague alarms that told her to leave, but also made her that much more curious.

They walked up the stairs and past a black curtain into a dimly lit room. Inside were frames of various sizes and shapes, each on an easel and covered with a sheet. Roy paused at the door as Jennifer circled the room. Something danced on the edge of her perception, tugging at her as she passed a small easel. It was a taste or perhaps a smell, she couldn't be sure. She smiled at the notion that it might be painted in chocolate and reached for the bottom of the sheet. She took a deep breath before lifting it, sensing this was something special. Then, with one smooth motion, she lifted the sheet up and tossed it over the frame.

"Is this a joke?" she asked, stepping back.

"Oh, it's no joke, I assure you," he said, his tone a bit condescending. "I did say they were challenging, did I not? Perhaps you're not up to it."

Jennifer tilted her head, puzzled. The frame bore no canvas, but rather a single panel of dark glass. Curiously, it offered no reflection. Light wholly disappeared within the frame.

"But it's blank," she said.

"Blank?" he said with jovial laugh. "Oh, no, it's far from empty."

"I'm interpreting the total lack of anything there as 'blank.' Maybe I just don't know art."

He just smiled. It was a patronizing smile, Jennifer thought, and it angered her. She started to walk away, but something stopped her. She *did* feel something there; something just beyond her grasp, a faint voice calling out from just beyond her periphery. It was a weird feeling and somewhat frightening. Once again her better judgment told her to leave. She planted her feet firmly and reached for the glass. Her fingertips brushed softly against the surface, finding it oddly warm.

Roy watched her closely. "Well?" he asked.

"Well, what? It's just. . . ."

Jennifer's words fell away as her body grew limp. The smells hit her first; chocolate, peanuts, and pine trees. The tastes followed; she could taste the cinnamon and candy bars. Then, like a TV channel coming into focus, she could feel the rest: the excitement of opening Christmas packages, the warmth of a fireplace, the smiles and comfort of a family together. Bright reds and greens saturated her senses. Her lips curled into a forced smile and her legs grew unsteady. This was no simulated perception; she experienced a rush of emotions and sensations that weren't her own, but no less genuine. Finally the flow subsided and she was released.

She struggled to regain her breath and stay on her feet. Roy watched her with a knowing smile but offered no help. Frightened, she ran down the stairs and out of the building.

The next day she walked back to the gallery, distracted by the lingering sensations from the day before. When she closed her eyes she could still see the brightly colored wrapping paper. She could hear the sound of a 45 RPM record playing on an old stereo. It was a song she had never heard before and now it echoed repeatedly in her head.

Preoccupied, she didn't recognize her freshman home room teacher until she had passed her.

"Mrs. Feldman!" she called. "It's me!"

"I'm sorry?" the woman answered.

"Jennifer Roma." She watched the woman, waiting for recognition. Perplexed when there was none, she added, "You taught freshmen geometry. You were my home room teacher!"

"No, you must have me mistaken," the woman answered. "I don't . . . I don't know you." The woman frowned, conflicted, and turned to walk away.

"You were at my brother's funeral," Jennifer said quietly as the woman disappeared around the corner.

"And what has you all troubled today, hmmm?" Roy asked as she entered the gallery.

"I just saw my favorite teacher outside," Jennifer said, puzzled, "but she didn't recognize me."

"Ah, it's a sad fact that students are sometimes not as important as they'd like to think," he said.

Unconvinced, Jennifer remained quiet. Instead, she gazed at the stairs leading to the private gallery.

Roy saw her gaze and smiled. "You've want to try another, to see if what you felt yesterday was real."

Jennifer didn't answer. She followed him up the stairs and looked around with apprehension.

"Take your pick," he said, casually flicking his hand.

She walked around, pausing at each painting before selecting a tall, narrow frame in the corner. Her heart pumped furiously. She took a deep breath and slowly pulled the sheet up. As with the day before, the frame held only absorbent glass. With a mixture of fear and anticipation, she reached toward the imageless work.

The sound of thunder cracked, booming in her ears. The distant glow of city lights illuminated her path. She had never been to Baltimore, but the skyline was now a familiar part of her life. Rain poured down her face and her breath wheezed as she ran, laughing. A man caught up to her and pulled her with little resistance to the soaked grass. She gazed into eyes that she had never seen before. She knew this man. She trusted him; loved him. They kissed again passionately, as they had all night. Finally he spoke the words that she had always known he would: "Marry me."

She trembled as the wave of a perfect moment washed over her. She laughed as she accepted, happier than she had even been in her life. The fresh smell of wet grass filled her nostrils. The warmth of his lips pressed against hers.

Slowly the reverie faded and she fell to the floor.

"That's . . . amazing," she said in a barely audible whisper.

"Yes," he said, helping her to her feet. "It is, isn't it."

"But I don't understand. I don't see anything there."

He snorted derisively. "Sight is the crudest of the senses. I deal in emotion."

"But how. . . ?"

He shook his head dismissively. "'How' is just technique, a means to an end. You want to know about technique, read a book. You want to know about art . . . then let yourself go, experience it."

An intoxicating mix of new sensations still danced in her head. It was more than an hour before she had regained her composure. Still a little shaky, she asked for another.

"Nice of you to actually join us." Her father's voice was quiet with anger, his eyes still intent on the morning paper.

"I was just going to grab some breakfast before I went out," Jennifer said, grabbing a slice of toast.

"Another day at your 'job?'" She knew that tone. Another fight was coming.

"I don't get it. You wanted me to find a job, so I found one. What do you want me to do now?"

"We wanted you to get a real job, not this . . . this 'art' thing. It was supposed to be a few hours a day; now you spend all day there and head straight to your room when you do deign to come home." Her father glared at her, anxious for another confrontation.

"Honey, you've been gone a lot and you're acting so strange. Is there something . . . you know, going on there with this person?" Her mother sat down at the table, the look of maternal compassion was out of place on her face.

Jennifer laughed. "Oh mom! This guy's like . . . three hundred pounds! It's just a job."

"We're just concerned about you, Jen. You've been so vulnerable since Jeff died."

"There's something not right about that place. I think we'd all be happier if you didn't work there any more," her father said.

"What? I'm nineteen, Dad. I can make my own decisions!"

"Not as long as you live under our roof." Signaling the conversation was closed, her father returned to his paper and locked the world out, as he had done every day since her brother's death.

Crisp autumn air swirled around her. Brown and orange leaves danced lazily in the wind. Bundled and warm, she ran across a yard that seemed endless. She tripped and fell into a pile of leaves, laughing. A tiny tongue lapped at her face. His name was Sparky. He rolled onto his back and she stroked his tummy, watching his tail thump the ground. She looked into his flat face and brown eyes and knew that this dog was her only friend in the whole wide world.

"Come on, Sparky," she said and jumped to her feet. She grabbed a small stick and threw it as hard as she could. Sparky took off in a leap as the stick bounced twice on the curb across the street. She laughed at the way his ears blew back as he ran. Then the screech of tires on hard asphalt slowed the world to a crawl. In painfully slow motion she watched Sparky's body roll under the front wheel of a car. In a blur, the dog was cradled in her arms, whimpering softly. Then its broken body grew still.

Jennifer sobbed on the floor as her fingers slipped away from the glass.

"Surprised at the intensity, eh?" He crouched beside her. "The painful emotions are often the deepest, you know. You harbor your own pain, yes?"

Jennifer couldn't respond. She simply stared at the glass, searching for a reflection that wasn't there.

"Of course you do. We all do." He sat down beside her. "What happened to your brother, Jennifer? You were with him when he died, weren't you."

"Yes," she said quietly.

"And that memory is vivid. So vivid it haunts your every waking hour."

"I couldn't save him," she said, tears now flowing freely. "We were on the lake, on a boat. I had . . . it was the first time he offered to share his drugs with me, some Oxy he'd bought. I didn't even know what they were, but he was . . . he was so smart and . . . I wanted to be like him."

"And then?" he prodded.

Suddenly Jennifer's tears stopped. She took a deep breath and said calmly, "And then he fell out of the boat. And I couldn't do anything but watch him sink."

They sat quietly for several minutes before either spoke again.

"It was your fault, Jennifer," he said softly. "If you had been stronger, your brother would be alive."

"I know," she whispered.

He paused, staring at her with forceful eyes until she couldn't meet his gaze. "I can make that pain go away."

She had expected this. "How?"

"Where do you think the memories in the glass came from? Moments of pain too difficult to bear or moments so joyful that life pales, becomes stagnant and bitter. All these moments, given to me freely."

"Like Mrs. Feldman," Jennifer said.

"An affair that ended badly and cost her her marriage. What worth is a memory, hmmm?" he continued.

"It's what makes us who we are," she replied.

"And what if we don't want to be that person?" he asked, moving closer to her. "What if the subtraction of one memory could free us to be the person we might have been?"

She tried to force away the image of her brother sliding silently below the water as they walked together past a curtain into another room. A single light bulb gave spare illumination. There was no chair, no table, nothing save for an easel with a frame.

She approached the easel, her steps devoured by the stillness of the room. As she approached the glass, she noticed her own reflection where there had previously been none. This glass was not dark like the rest. It ached to be filled. She realized then the answer to Roy's question.

"Pain and the joy are why we endure the numbness in between," she said aloud. "I was trying so hard to block out one that I ignored the other. It's time I learned to accept both. I can't give my pain away. That would just make me empty, not better."

She turned to leave but Roy blocked her path. "I'm sorry Jennifer. Yours is simply too strong a memory to pass up."

He grabbed her by the wrist and pulled her toward the glass. Struggling against his bulk was futile. As he forced her hand close to the glass, she kicked hard at his shin. He let out a sharp curse of pain as his leg crumpled beneath him and began to fall toward her. Twisting out of the way, she could only watch helplessly as his left hand fell against the glass, still clutching her own hand in his right.

Fire crackled beside them. Loud pops coincided with sharp flashes that illuminated the cavernous room, home to so many wonders.

"But why? Why would you destroy the glass?" Roy pleaded.

"Because, Roy, what it does is wrong."

"But it's . . . wondrous!" He had been lucky to stumble across the workshop, even luckier to convince the craftsman there to take him as apprentice. But he demanded so many menial tasks of Roy; work that was beneath him.

The man sighed and turned to face Roy. "I should never have shown you the secret of the dark glass. It extracts too great a price for the experience it stores. It leaves people hollow, incomplete. No, Roy, when I shatter the glass, the memories will return to their rightful place. We have much to atone for, I'm afraid."

Roy watched as the man turned his back and prepared to destroy the extraordinary glass. A rage grew within him. He could not allow such phenomenon to be extinguished. He grabbed the iron poker from the fireplace and brought it swiftly down upon the artist's head. He spun around to face Roy, astonishment in his eyes. The trickle of blood slid lazily down his forehead as he tried to remain standing. Roy found violence loathsome, but he would make an exception this one time. Best to get the unpleasantness over with quickly, he thought, and swung the poker again and again until the man before him no longer resembled a man. Breathing in labored gulps, he dropped the poker to the floor.

The realization of what he had done was overwhelming. But the glass was worth it. The delicious wealth of experience it offered was worth any price. It was the only thing that mattered to him as he set about the task of disposing of the body of his mentor.

Jennifer's hand slipped from his grasp and she fell to the floor, drained. When her senses returned, she saw Roy, laying beside her in a fetal ball, his blank eyes nearly devoid of life. She was repulsed by what she had experienced.

"If this is taken from you, would you be any less vile? If the act goes unremembered, is it any less heinous? And to think, I actually considered your offer."

He gave no acknowledgement that he could hear her. He simply stared forward vacantly.

"What will happen to those whose memories you raped when I break the glass?" she said. "What will happen when the tragedies and ecstasies of their lives come rushing back? I guess we'll find out."

She walked past the curtain, to the outer room. She picked up a large glass, carefully holding it by the frame only. She held it over her head and paused before sending it crashing to the floor.

"Is the fat man okay?" The little girl pointed at Roy, but was quickly scolded by her mother.

The clearance sale was going well. With only a few pieces remaining, there would be enough money to pay for Roy's care. After all, he was now incapable of caring for himself. Even her parents seemed satisfied at how well she had taken over the liquidation of the gallery. Perhaps she had found a calling after all.

"I'm sorry," the mother said as she walked up to Jennifer. "Madelyn just says whatever pops into her brain."

"It's okay," Jennifer said. "Trust me, he doesn't take offense."

"It must be nice," the woman continued, "just pushing a broom all day. He doesn't seem to have a care in the world. Except . . . he keeps sweeping the same section of floor."

Jennifer thought for a moment before answering. "Well, you know, sometimes one person's mercy is another's purgatory."

Roy continued to sweep back and forth, oblivious to his surroundings. He paused and looked around, confused. Something eluded him, like the buzzing of an unseen insect. With a shake of his head, he ignored it and went about his cleaning. Only with great effort did he move away from the spot he repeatedly cleaned. But he would return. Jennifer knew that as a certainty. For above him, mounted just out of reach on the wall was a large frame with a single, unbroken sheet of glass.

~

David Seigler *is a repeat offender in the* Triangulation *anthologies, placing "Graveyard of the Cloud Gods" in last year's volume. His work also appears in* All Possible Worlds *and* Neo-opsis Magazines. *He lives in Texas with his wife and multiple children where he sells comic books and occasionally writes short science fiction. You can learn more at www.groundzerocomics.com/DavidSeigler.htm.*

Souls on Display

Kurt Kirchmeier

We were playing road hockey when I broke Mr. Mandoka's soul. It had been hanging in his living room window, strung from the curtain rod as though it were a sun-catcher. Which, I suppose, it sort of was; it certainly shattered like glass.

I'd known it was there, of course; we all did. In fact, we often joked about accidentally breaking it, about how bad we would feel if we did—robbing him of the afterlife and all. Still, I never imagined it would actually happen. Hard as my slap shots were, they were generally pretty accurate.

My friends just stared in the seconds that followed, their eyes wide with disbelief. Billy's mouth dropped open, his huge wad of gum falling to the street. Billy was always chewing gum, and never just one piece, either. It was the whole pack or none at all.

"Old Man Mandoka's gonna kill you," he said. Chris and Evan nodded sagely behind him, the graphite shafts of their hockey sticks gleaming under the cold winter sun.

"Old Man Mandoka couldn't kill a fly," Evan's little brother piped in. "He can hardly even walk."

It was true; Mr. Mandoka *was* pretty old. However, having seen the size of the head on his cane, I couldn't help but feel a little bit anxious.

Jenna—the only girl on the block brave enough to play with us—shook her head. "Stupid," she remarked. "Why'd he have it hanging in the window anyway?"

It was a question we'd been asking both each other and ourselves for as long as I could remember. Why would *anyone* hang their soul in their window? Not only was it risky in the extreme but scandalous as well. Everyone knew that.

Well, everyone but Mr. Mandoka, it seemed.

I left the others to ponder the question and ambled on up the driveway, unable to avert my gaze from the small bit of soul still hanging from the rod, spinning around and around on its string like the broken tip of a Christmas bulb.

Mr. Mandoka wasn't home; we'd paused our game about a half-hour before to let his Caddy through. Nevertheless, my stomach sank as I sidled up to the window and peered in.

It was worse than I'd feared.

The soul (what was left of it) was scattered all across the living room floor, some in chunks the size of my fist, others in fragments no bigger than a marble—roughly the size that the entire thing would have been at birth, or so my mother often told me. I hated when she said that. The last image I wanted was that of my soul covered in afterbirth. I pushed the thought away and continued surveying the damage.

Though I'd seen it in its entirety many times, albeit from a distance, I'd never realized just how pretty Mr. Mandoka's soul had been, color-wise, I mean: frosted lilac. Mine was green, and a putrid shade at that. I'd always hated it.

Fat Sam (he was actually a bean-pole) joined me at the window, followed immediately thereafter by the others. Jenna whistled low, and then loudly smacked her gum (Billy had a crush on her, so sometimes he would share).

"What're you gonna do?" asked Shamus, who was the oldest of our crew.

I shrugged. Given the circumstances, I was pretty sure a simple "I'm sorry" wasn't going to cut it.

"Wait, I guess," I replied. What else was I supposed to do, run? It wasn't as if I'd stolen a crab apple from the guy's tree (that was the day before); I'd broken his soul for crying out loud, his one and only connection to the afterlife, his boarding ticket to paradise. The least I could do was stick around and explain to him how it happened, that it wasn't on purpose.

"We still gonna play hockey?" Evan asked after a moment of awkward silence.

Jenna gave him a shove and called him an idiot, then stood there shaking her head. Evan had never been the sharpest knife in the drawer. More like a spoon, actually.

The eight of us milled around for a while on the snow-dusted lawn, none of us really knowing what to say. I could sense that the others wanted to leave but didn't have the heart to let me take the blame alone.

"It's okay guys," I finally said, tossing them a bone. "You can go. I'm the one who broke it."

"You sure?" asked Billy. I nodded. He shrugged, then immediately turned to Jenna, sensing an opportunity now that his afternoon had just freed up. "Wanna come over for hot chocolate?" he asked her.

She moved her head from side to side, as though weighing her options. "Okay," she finally agreed. I think Billy was beginning to win her over.

The others took their leave shortly thereafter, wishing me luck before filing away one by one. Fat Sam was the last to go. He gave me a reassuring punch on the shoulder and told me he would look on eBay when he got home.

I nodded and smiled, knowing that we could never afford to buy Mr. Mandoka a new one. Besides, there was really no proof that someone else's soul—even if they'd willingly signed it over—could grant you passage to the afterlife. The general consensus was that it wouldn't. Fat Sam, of course, knew all this himself; he was just trying to make me feel better. He stopped at the end of the drive and looked back over his shoulder.

"Chin up," he said. Fat Sam always said that. I smiled again. I really was lucky to have such good friends.

Mr. Mandoka arrived home a short time later, his freshly washed Caddy shining brilliantly as it meandered up the drive. I swallowed hard and got up from the step, my hands shaking, my knees weak.

He sat there in his car for a moment, giving me a suspicious look. Then, as though he'd sensed it rather than seen it, his gaze shifted to the shattered living room window, where it remained for several long seconds. Finally he got out of the car, leaning on his cane as he stood.

"It was an accident," I quickly said and motioned toward the net on the curb. "We were playing hockey and, well, I kinda missed." I was speaking fast, sort of a half stutter.

He stood staring at the window. "Missed, huh?"

I immediately regretted my choice of words. I looked down at my shoes, my cheeks burning in spite of the wintry air. "I'll pay for it," I finally said. "The window, I mean." It was a poor excuse for restitution, I knew, but I didn't really have anything else to offer.

Mr. Mandoka nodded, jowls bouncing like miniature saddlebags. He joined me at the bottom of the steps, his face expressionless. "You know how to use a staple-gun?" he said.

A staple-gun? Confusion tied my tongue in a temporary knot, so I merely nodded like the idiot I felt.

"Well, c'mon then," he replied, motioning for me to follow.

He led me down to his basement and, after a short search through a cluttered storage room, handed me a roll of clear plastic wrap, the sort often used to cut down on draft. He then set me to work, saying not a word about his soul.

Plastic wrap for the inside, quarter-inch plywood for the outside: my fingers were freezing by the time I finished, my gloves offering little in the way of insulation against the cold steel of the staple-gun. Mr. Mandoka inspected my work with wordless scrutiny.

Apparently satisfied that it would stand the test, he invited me back inside. He'd taken a shop-vac to the living room carpet while I was working, sucking up his soul as though it were soil from an overturned plant. He sat me down at his kitchen table in front of a steaming mug of hot cocoa, which I immediately wrapped my hands around.

"I appreciate you sticking around like you did," he said as he took a chair opposite me. "Most boys would've run off."

I smiled somewhat guiltily, for it wasn't like I hadn't thought about it, albeit only briefly. "You probably would have found out anyway."

"Even so," he said, "it shows responsibility. You've a heck of a work ethic, too." He gestured vaguely toward the living room.

I shrugged. "I help my dad in the shop sometimes."

"Is that so?" he said and looked at me strangely then, as if struck by a sudden thought. His eyes narrowed in silent appraisal, though what exactly he might be appraising me for, I hadn't the faintest idea. I shifted uncomfortably in my chair, pretending like I didn't notice.

"So is there anything else I can do?" I asked him. The one simple task he'd set before me, while not at all pleasant, did little to assuage my guilt. And the fact that the old man was being so nice to me didn't help, either. Part of me wanted him to rage, to get it all out in one shot and have done with it. That's what my dad would have done.

"Hmm," he said, again with the hard look of consideration. "Perhaps there is. Tell me, have you ever had a job?"

"I had a paper route once," I said. "Does that count?"

"I'd say so," he replied. "Did you like it?"

I shrugged. "It was okay, I guess."

He rubbed his chin thoughtfully. "Well, what would you say if I offered you a different sort of job?" He held up his cane. "Can't move around like I used to. Could use me an assistant."

"Assistant?" I said. "For what?"

He smiled. "C'mon, I'll show you."

I followed him out the back door, inwardly reeling at the strange turn of events. I'd just broken his soul, and now he was offering me a job?

We stopped at the side of his garage, whereupon he drew a giant set of keys from his pocket and fumbled through them one by one, mumbling all the while about how they all looked the same.

"Here we are," he finally said. "Get ready now, this might seem a little odd at first glance." That said, he opened the door and then reached around the corner to turn on a light.

"Odd" could not have been more of an understatement.

The entire side of the far wall was covered with souls in sizes ranging from baseballs to breadboxes. They were hanging from hooks and sitting on shelves. A couple of them, the bigger ones, were dangling from the rafters above. The shapes and colors were as varied as the sizes. Some of them were round and blue, some triangular and fiery red. Others were similar to my own: bulbous and misshapen, like pillow lava hardened beneath the sea. There was one in the corner so dark a purple it looked almost black.

I stood gaping on the threshold.

Mr. Mandoka chuckled. "It isn't what you think," he said and motioned towards the souls with his chin. "I made these. They're replicas."

"Replicas?"

"Indeed," he said, and then with a wink, "and so was the one you broke, so you needn't fret about it any longer. I regret to say that my real one's been gone for quite some time. Took a tumble down the stairs, must have been, oh, twenty years back now."

I stared at him, unblinking, stunned, and relieved all at once.

"But how?" I finally managed. "What're they made of?"

"Glass," Mr. Mandoka said.

I took a step inside, only then noticing the furnace in the corner, along with all the tools strewn about the place, most of which in no way resembled anything I'd ever seen my dad use. I glanced at Mr. Mandoka, who was now standing in the center of the workshop, leaning on his cane.

"What do you do with them?" I asked.

"Sell them," he said. "Most of the time, anyway. Some are just practice pieces."

"Sell them to who?"

He shrugged. "People like myself. Those who've broken their own. Happens more often than you think, you know. Broken souls, I mean. You just don't hear about it is all. Heck, there's probably a half-dozen on this street alone."

I raised an eyebrow in surprise. I often eavesdropped on my mother and her friends as they gossiped over tea, so I was always up on things as far as the neighborhood was concerned. I couldn't recall anyone having ever mentioned a broken soul before, much less a half dozen.

"But why?" I asked. "What good is a fake one?"

"Peace of mind," he replied. "You ever been to a funeral?"

I nodded. "My aunt Mary died two months ago."

"So you saw her soul, then, at the front of the church?"

Barring wishes to the contrary, a soul was always displayed during a funeral and then placed in the coffin just prior to burial, where it would continue to shrink until finally there was no trace of it whatsoever. Only then would the spirit have fully moved on.

I nodded again. I remembered my aunt's soul well. It looked like something out of a Picasso painting.

"And was it her real soul, or just a replica?"

I made as if to speak, but then stopped myself. "Beats me," I said after a momentary pause. "I never really thought about it."

"Exactly," Mr. Mandoka replied. "Most people wouldn't. That's why I sell them, so families don't end up worrying needlessly. Like I said, peace of mind."

"So they don't tell their families? About them being broken?"

Mr. Mandoka shook his head. "Not usually, no."

"Isn't that dishonest, letting them think that they're going to heaven when they're not?"

"How do you know they don't go to heaven?"

"How could they?"

Mr. Mandoka smiled. I got the distinct impression that he'd had this conversation before.

"What do you think heaven is?" he said.

I shrugged. "I don't know. Whatever I want it to be, I guess."

"Precisely," he said. "Whatever you want it to be. Now let's assume that your best friend. . . ." He waited for me to fill in the name.

"Billy," I provided.

"Okay. Now let's assume that Billy ends up breaking his soul and that you don't; so you carry on up to heaven, and he goes to . . . wherever it is he goes to. If heaven really is whatever you want it to be, then wouldn't you want Billy to be there with you?"

I turned the notion over a few times before replying. "I never thought about it like that before."

"Not many people do," Mr. Mandoka replied. "Not many people do."

"So it doesn't matter?" I asked. "Whether it gets broken?" It pretty much went against everything I'd ever been taught, both in church as well as school. Strangely enough, though, it made sense. At least to me it did.

Mr. Mandoka shrugged. "Maybe, maybe not. Perhaps we're just born with them so that we know that something else exists. Something to base our faith on, I guess you could say. Then again, perhaps it's just God's way of telling us that life is fragile and that we should make the best of it while we have it." He shrugged again. "It's a mystery. The way I figure it, as long as you've lived a moral life, and as long as you've got people around who want you by their side after it ends, you'll always have a place in heaven. It just might not be your own."

I began my apprenticeship three days later, starting with the easy stuff: sorting cullet (raw glass), heating pipes, making newspaper pads, and preparing tools. Mr. Mandoka, meanwhile, explained to me the various techniques and finer points of the trade. Glass blowing, some might have called it, but Mr. Mandoka referred to it as "soul-forging."

By and large, the work was tedious. I often spent hours on end with the customers beforehand, meticulously reconstructing their souls from whatever fragments and shards he or she had brought with them to the shop—can't very well make a replica without seeing the original, after all.

It was during this time that Mr. Mandoka usually imparted his philosophy regarding the afterlife to the clients: "The Many Heavens Theory," as he called it. I soon discovered he was as much a counselor as he was a journeyman.

I also discovered why he'd had his own soul hanging in the window. It was a calling card of sorts, a mark of the trade. Only a privileged few knew of its meaning, and it was they who directed others to the shop.

I continued playing hockey with the gang on the weekends, attributing my evening absences to a restoration project that Mr. Mandoka had me helping him with in restitution for my blunder. I told them the old man and I were rebuilding a Model-T roadster. None of them were the wiser. Not at first, at least.

It was only months later, after Fat Sam confided to me that he had accidentally shattered his own soul while taking it down from his closet, that I began to let my friends in on my secret. By this time, I had graduated from general shop duties and was learning about some of the more advanced aspects of the job, such as thread-wrapping and color application.

In light of my newfound skills, I took it upon myself to make Fat Sam's my first solo project. Mr. Mandoka coached me, of course, but only by verbal means. As far as hands-on labor was concerned, it was all me. When I presented the finished creation to Sam a couple weeks later, he couldn't even tell the difference.

Nor, for that matter, could Billy, several weeks after that.

He arrived on my doorstep on a sunny Sunday morning, garbage bag in hand, chagrin on his face.

"What happened?" I said.

He shrugged, clearly embarrassed at the thought of relating the tale. Nevertheless, after persistent prodding on my part, he finally coughed it up.

"I dropped it in the bathtub," he said.

I narrowed my eyes. "Why did you have it in the bathtub?"

He shrugged again. "I was cleaning it."

"Why?" Although I dusted my own from time to time, I'd never really given any consideration to actually scrubbing it spotless. Why bother? It wasn't like I ever showed it to anyone. Billy looked the other way, his cheeks flushed. It was then that it hit me.

"You dog!" I said. "You were gonna show it to Jenna, weren't you?" They had become an item during the initial phase of my apprenticeship and had since been making the rest of us sick with all their "honey" this and "sweetie" that. I was happy for them, though—perhaps even a little bit jealous.

"I gotta know," he replied. "You know?"

I nodded and left it at that. We'd all heard stories about soul mates.

Billy's soul proved quite a challenge, one that I couldn't help but laugh over. I might have guessed it would resemble a giant wad of well-chewed bubblegum.

In the months and years that followed—fulfilling ones, for the most part —Mr. Mandoka became somewhat of a second father to me, so when he finally passed away—just days after my high school graduation—I found myself left with not only a cozy little bungalow and garage/soul-forge but also a profound sense of sadness. Long since estranged from whatever family he had left in the world (the reason, I'll never know), Mr. Mandoka had bequeathed almost all of his worldly possessions to me, his only stipulation being that I continue with the work.

And so I did.

By the time I turned twenty-eight, I had replaced not only Fat Sam's and Billy's souls but also my own. I still worry from time to time, but then I find myself surrounded by those I love and can't help but believe that we'll all have our place in heaven. It just might not be our own.

In the meantime, I've got my new soul hanging in my window, strung from the curtain rod as though it were a sun-catcher.

~

This story originally appeared in the GlassFire *anthology.*

Kurt Kirchmeier *is proudly Canadian, happily married, and currently in the process of finishing a pair of novels aimed at younger readers. His fiction has appeared in a variety of places including* Kaleidotrope, Shimmer, *and* Triangulation: End of Time, *and is forthcoming in* TOTU, Weird Tales, *and elsewhere. When he isn't writing, Kurt enjoys doing digital artwork and shooting stick at the local pool hall. For more information visit www.kurtkirchmeier.com.*

A More Beautiful Monster

Loretta Sylvestre

When the sorcerer DuHarren put the knife in my hand, the silver hilt stung cold against my flesh. His grey eyes glinted steel and ice, yet they held mine fast as surely as Hell binds a sinner's soul. It was I, though, who burned with God's vengeance.

The sound of hooves hurrying over cobbles and splashing through slush reminded me that outside a storm raged, hard rain tattered by wind like a dying breath of winter. But within DuHarren's chambers, hearth fire and gas light gleamed off polished wealth, and his bare chest glistened with moisture in the still heat.

He pointed precisely to a place on the faultless curve of his breast. "Just here," he said. "This is where you must strike. Do you understand Father Michael?"

His brazen behavior taunted me, fanned my wrath. I raised my eyes to his, remembering that, only days ago, I had seen something in those eyes worth redeeming. Now, I found in them only pride and malevolence.

"Yes," I whispered. "Oh yes, I understand." I raised the blade between us, but stopped, stood frozen for a hard instant while rivulets of sweat beaded on DuHarren's murderous hands—and on mine. It gleamed liquid red in the firelight—like blood, like pools of it cooling beneath Mary Evans' corpse.

"Mr. DuHarren," Mary Evans said to me, and though I nodded encouragingly, she lowered her eyes and returned to silence.

Those were the first words she'd addressed to me in the five long minutes since I'd ushered her into my office. I'd poured us both hot, sweet tea, and tried to make her comfortable, but still she perched on the edge of the settee, twiddling her fingers in her lap as if to loosen courage like yarn for knitting.

I sipped at my tea, then put the cup on the saucer with a harsher clink than I'd intended. Seeing the girl's lip tremble, I curbed impatience. Every soul in the city had heard of DuHarren the Sorcerer, who haunted the banks of the River DuSaunt stealing souls for Satan by the dark of the moon. I did no such thing, and though the Demon Tamuel was my long-time associate,

I'd never met Satan and cherished hope never to do so. Still, the fearful notion had been planted in childhood, and Mary was having a difficult time shaking it.

The girl knew what service I could provide, of course, or she wouldn't have come. She'd likely sought the advice of some crone who'd told her that I could—for a price—undo the choice she now regretted and unravel its consequences. I knew already the nature of that regret, it was plainly written in her age, her station, the dread in her eyes, and the flush on her cheeks. But I could do nothing until she overcame her ingrained fears, confessed, and requested my help.

I wished heartily that she'd find her voice, but I'd been a Sorcerer—or more precisely a Revisionist—for a very long time, and experience had taught me that this moment couldn't be rushed. Trying a proven tactic, I rose and—as if her words and silence were both far from my mind—began to arrange wood on the fire.

She spoke to my back. "I'm pregnant, Mr. DuHarren."

She would want to undo her decision to receive her lover, and she would want to accomplish the Revision quickly, believing we could manage it before her condition started to show. Despite two-and-a-half centuries of Tamuel's influence, I continued to strive for kindness—or at least courtesy— so I didn't tell her that it was already much too late for that. Surely every cook and strumpet in town had already divined her pregnancy and shuttled the news about in whispers.

I settled back in my chair, glanced up briefly, and said with indifference, "Please go on, Mary."

"I'm not . . . I've not been wed." She cringed as she looked up, plainly fearing violent condemnation, yet her eyes begged for a chance to explain.

I granted her a sympathetic look.

"Davey and I plan to wed, sir, we do. But he's called for service in the regiment, and it's a chance he'd never looked for at all. His family . . . they're respectable but poorer than my own, even, and it was only . . . it's the greatest good luck, Mr. DuHarren. It wouldn't be prudent to wed now." She looked at her hands, watching them clutch the homespun that covered her knees.

"Why is that, Mary? If you wed and he's lost in battle, spirits forbid, you'll at least have a widow's pension."

"I have thought of it, but. . . . Sir, I'm afraid that if Davey knows, he won't go at all. If he were to trade his one chance to make his way because of this, I couldn't forgive myself."

"Should your Davey perhaps have a choice?"

I'd spoken mildly, but even my well-practiced calm was shaken by her vehement response.

"No, sir!" She sat bolt upright, her countenance transformed. "No, I'll not let him choose! What choice is there, Mr. DuHarren? If it's not the regiment then Davey must be thief or fisherman, and in either case the chance that he'll live to see the child grow up is far worse than his chance to reach a soldier's pension."

Tamuel flared into my perception, looming suddenly over the girl with hard-breathing desire. Her unexpected passion inflamed him. *This one,* his attitude said, *I want.* He would own her, command her, use her up body and soul—the price of our service, should she seal the contract. The Demon stood at her shoulder and whispered through his teeth, compounding lies and truth in the dark halls of her mind, where fear and anger might render the mixture volatile.

My own temper rose but I shoved it down, laid refusal over it with the weight of stone. I would not feed Tamuel's flame. It had been a long time since anyone had come seeking my services who had not already been buried in moral filth. Long years had passed since compassion had roused me to resist his desires. I could not, by my pact, refuse service should a customer insist. But I could—at some later cost to myself—try to dissuade.

I had no qualms about unmaking the pregnancy. In thirteen score years, I'd seen enough to understand that, sometimes, for a woman to simply not be pregnant remained the best solution for all—even the child. The choice always weighed heavy on a woman; the price was high, regardless of the means by which she accomplished the deed. But Mary had come to me. She'd garnered Tamuel's interest. The cost to her, measured in pain, would soar to sickening heights.

I couldn't let it happen.

When she began to speak again, Tamuel's sick, selfish thinking colored her words. Her voice grew strident. "And then, what of me? I'm Lady Warwick's personal maid. It was hard work that got me my position—and bootlicking, and incredible luck. If I'm wed, I can't be her maid, and if I'm pregnant I'll be lucky if the Estate keeps me on as a char-woman."

Tamuel's sparks reflected in Mary's eyes, witness to the inroads he'd made toward her soul. I took an iron grip on the moment, calling up reserves of strength I'd almost forgotten I owned. Ignoring Tamuel's warning growls, I placed my hands on Mary Evans' shoulders and spoke with cool persuasion.

"Mary, this Revision you seek, despite your intention, draws on darkness. I'll not allow it until you've considered consequences. Look at me." I spoke the command in the manner of Mesmer, and when she obeyed, I held her gaze until her hazel eyes went still and her breathing slowed.

"Now look into the fire, Mary Evans. Tell me what you see."

It was a parlor trick, but if it worked she would think it magic. She would encounter her fears and find her own wisdom in the flames, and take it for vision.

The door snapped shut behind Mary's heavy skirts and I laid my palms flat against the oak, leaning into it and letting relief loosen my stiff shoulders. *Thank God,* I thought, and felt more than heard Tamuel's answering snarl. I paid his temper no mind. I felt grateful, recompensed as I could not remember having felt any time in the last decade. Who was to be thanked for such a gift if not God?

Mary Evans had seen, as I'd hoped she would. She'd gazed into the flames and understood what she would lose—far beyond the precious life of her child—if she insisted on Revision. A glimpse of the true cost had been enough to open her ears, and she'd heard her heart's plea for mercy. When she cried, I'd fed her cakes and dried fruit and gave her sweet, milky tea. She'd left my rooms restored; sad, but brave and content.

Moments such as this, moments of relief from a triple lifetime's burden of guilt and dread came to me so rarely that—for all my hard earned strength and power—I trembled as I turned away from the door, and nearly fell to my knees in tears if not in prayer. A long minute later, I passed a hand over my burning eyes and walked back to my chair by the fire. The flames had faded to a tender glow.

"This calls for brandy," I said aloud to break the mood, and reached for the decanter. The Demon howled displeasure, but disturbed my peace not an iota. "No, Tamuel," I said. "She chose, as is her right. I've turned her from your Hell's gate, and by our pact I've won twelve hours of peace before you extract your toll. Tonight I'll sleep without your hot breath on my neck. Leave me."

Tamuel complied. He had no choice, being as firmly bound as I by the terms of our contract. But as he withdrew, he growled something I'd long expected but that nevertheless chilled my spine.

"DuHarren," he said, "I've grown quite tired of you."

The next morning, Tuesday, Tamuel remained absent long after my contracted twelve hours of freedom, but my peace was shattered by a visit from a young priest. I had breakfasted at leisure, and was standing near my windows watching sunbeams break and scatter over the city when a hansom cab stopped in the street below. The Father, a small, fair man with a blaze of red hair and a light step, advanced on my door, his manner brisk despite the weight of a thick black cross hanging at his chest over the brown wool of his cassock.

Briefly, I considered ignoring his knock, but there would be little point. Others of his kind had come before, and over the decades I'd learned that young priests are unfailingly persistent. Not that I could fault them for that. Church and Sorcery make poor neighbors, and truth be told I myself held little pride in my art—so little that deliberately I'd taken no apprentice. When finally death released me, I'd be the last of my kind. I'd take cool comfort in that as I burned and choked on sulfur.

Be that as it may, no man wishes to take up lodgings in Hell any sooner than needs must, so as I swung open my office door, I braced myself against holy assault.

"Good morning," he began. "My name is Father Michael, from St. Martin's Church." To his credit, he nearly hid his fear that in meeting me he might come face-to-face with the Devil, though he gave in to the urge to finger the rosary hanging at his hip.

"State your business, Father." I pointedly did not invite him in.

The priest's freckled cheeks blushed crimson but he spoke slowly and managed an even tone. "I've heard stories about you since I was a boy, DuHarren. Until recently, I believed they were just that, wild tales and no more. But you are indeed flesh and bone I see, and lately your name arises among my flock. I want the truth, firsthand. Are you what they say you are?"

"If they say I'm a sorcerer, then yes. I'm the Revisionist, and the undoing of past events simply can't be done without sorcery." I smiled, but his youthful brow dipped into a baffled V, and in his gaze I caught both fear and —oddly—hope.

Repenting my inhospitality, I ushered him inside and offered the armchair. "Will you take tea?"

He smiled and began a nod of acceptance, then seemed to catch himself out. "Er . . . no, thank you. I'm quite comfortable." Giving the lie to those words he sat stiffly, only his eyes mobile as they roved over my polished wood and Turkish carpets. "Your business thrives."

"Yes," I smiled. "My customers are willing to pay dearly for my services. The magic I offer is a beautiful *seeming* thing. My clients almost never see danger until it's far too late." I told him at some length about my art, even provided him with examples of the kinds of things a young and vital priest might wish undone.

For a time he was silent, then he shook his head—a small, private gesture. "No sorcery partakes of beauty," he said. Brave words, but so soft that they nearly vanished in the hearth's whispering flames.

I began to pace, troubled—or perhaps intrigued. His sea-green eyes tracked my movements, and I watched him in return, keeping his tense figure in the corner of my eye as I traced and retraced the same four steps. He wore his crosses and beads like armor. The leather purse at his belt surely held testament and water, oil and salt. Yet, for all his talismans, I could see—I knew beyond doubt—that his God remained distant, scarcely more than a concept. He failed even to perceive the nearness of the Demon Tamuel, who at that very moment hovered behind his chair.

Tamuel laughed. I could feel his excitement, and I knew the cause. The Demon saw in our guest the same dissonance that vibrated in my senses. The young priest had ventured into battle unsure of his steel. His sword of faith might bend.

Offered a pretty evil, Father Michael could be subverted.

Arrayed—and armored I thought—with priestly instruments, I knocked on the sorcerer's door. "I'm Father Michael," I said, but the man was not at all what I'd expected, and it unsettled me so that I could scarcely hear him, let alone speak.

Civil though he seemed, I knew DuHarren was heathen, an abomination to God and Satan's servant. I refused to doubt that truth, yet very soon after I met him a strange and persistent image came to mind. Two DuHarrens, it seemed, paced before me. One reflected dark, the other light.

He's possessed, I thought, *in the truest sense.* But perhaps he could be saved. Perhaps an ember of humanity still burned within the Demon-clad heart. This flash of insight seemed god-given to me alone, and inspired by that belief and a nascent vision of what might be, I ignored the instruction of the church to take such matters to the Bishop. God chose me for this task, and I would see it done.

I stripped my ebony cross from around my neck, thrust it before me and, nearly shouting in my excitement, commenced the sacred rite of exorcism. "Have you, DuHarren, entered into a blood pact with the Devil and do you now repent?"

DuHarren's eyes widened and he smiled, incredulous. "What?"

"Have you entered—"

"I heard you, Father."

I rushed on, convincing myself that the rite might be effective without repentance on the part of the afflicted. "I exorcise thee, oh impious Satan," I began. "I abjure thee, by him who expelled thee from thy stronghold, bereft thee . . ." I trailed off as DuHarren, mocking theatrically, began to recite the formula himself.

". . . bereft thee of the arms which thou didst trust in, and distributed thy spoils." He turned his iron-grey eyes on me, chortling. "Come, priest," he said. "Why have you stopped? Must I recite the whole text alone?"

While I stood dumbstruck, DuHarren laughed until tears trailed down his cheeks. At length and with obvious effort he contained his mirth and flopped into an armchair.

He clutched his side and spoke between labored breaths. "Forgive me, Father Michael. I've heard it before once or twice. Besides, have you ever faced a Demon? I can't help but wonder what you'd do if one were to show himself." He fought another swell of laughter, and then shook his head and fell quiet.

I was watching his face closely—I couldn't seem to look away—and at that moment, all at once youth drained away and left him looking old in spirit and somber, as if he drew sadness from some deep, ancient well.

"Come, now," he said, and his voice was truly gentle. "I've been unkind. Put away your cross and save your salt and holy water for another time. Let's have tea."

While he busied himself with cups and saucers and spoons, I struggled to convince myself that I mustn't take tea with the Devil's man, tried to muster the drive to get up and leave. Instead, I did just as he had suggested: stowed away my cross and then sat silent, sipping sweet, clove-scented brew and contemplating sorcerer's flames.

DuHarren didn't break the silence until it had grown old and somehow comfortable. He reached over, then, and laid a hand on my shoulder as if to console me.

"Don't feel badly about this, Father," he said. "More experienced men than you have failed to save my soul. You are a bold and brave soldier of God and that should be rewarded. Here's what I offer: You may ask any three questions—two now, and the final one in three days. I'll answer with the truth."

My first question surprised me, coming immediately to my tongue as if it had lain in wait behind my teeth. "How does your magic work?"

DuHarren's answer droned on for some time, a lecture more tedious than any I'd endured at seminary. In the end all I retained was that it had to do with the nature of time, the nature of spirits, and the price of promises, services, and souls in Hell's markets.

I thought I would ask then whether the gossips spoke truth when they said DuHarren had been born before their grandmothers, but before I spoke, I read the answer in his eyes. Instead, I asked, "How have you lived so long?"

"I cannot die," DuHarren answered, in a voice that seemed tight with well-worn pain. "I can't die until I have a successor, and I won't name one. Thus, I go on living." He paused and his mouth toyed with the idea of a smile. Suddenly, his eyes sparkled, and he cocked an eyebrow, clearly teasing.

"Day after day," he said, "year upon year."

By Thursday evening, I'd sunk deeper into fatigue than I'd known was possible. I'd not slept for more than minutes at a time since my ill-fated attempt at exorcising DuHarren, two long days ago. My mind returned to that visit again and again, and every time I cursed my ineptitude, yet still I could not bring myself to take the problem to the bishop. And—like running barbed wire through every waking minute—I fretted over the choice of my third question.

As if it meant salvation.

I was grossly out of sorts by the time I entered the confessional. While I should have been preparing myself to hear the sins of my flock, the name DuHarren wound through my thoughts and chafed like rope. The overheated booth, with its hard seat and residue of a century's shame offered no comfort and did nothing to put me in a frame of mind to counsel sinners.

In less than an hour I learned more about my congregation than I'd ever wanted to know. Tim Garrett had confessed to coveting his neighbor, which the Ten Commandments didn't address at all. Donnell Jamison reported that he'd smashed his wife's wrist when she tried to stop him from pawning her dead mother's jewelry for whiskey funds—a cruelty, but not mentioned in scripture. And Millie Baker, surprise, admitted to having spread her legs even wider than usual for a bag of John Dempsey's stolen coppers.

The thought took root that my priesthood was farce. I wondered—not for the first time—whether my calling had ever been real. Had I merely taken my lucky chance and set out on the only road I could see that might lead out of poverty?

The question remained unanswerable, and I put it aside. I reminded each supplicant of the righteous path, prayed with them, assigned them penance which at least would assuage the conscience, and granted them absolution. As if it mattered.

Then Bailey Swanson came in, good man that he was.

He confessed that he'd obliged his aged, long-crippled mother when, after a final stroke she'd begged him to end her suffering. I remained mute for so long that finally Bailey curled his work-callused fingers through the partition screen and cried, "Well then, am I damned to Hell?" I thought *probably so,* but I choked out words of comfort, assigned meaningless penance, and sent the man on his way with absolution—mine, if not God's.

One more, I decided. Father Paulo would have to relieve me. I needed food and quiet, perhaps prayer or meditation, and definitely sleep—even if I had to seek a remedy from the herb-wife to get it. I cleared my throat as Mary Evans knelt and began her, "Forgive me father . . ."

This one should be easy, I thought. *She's a levelheaded girl.*

But as she poured out her miserable tale, I became first perplexed and then enraged—so much so that I could scarcely contain it. Of their own accord my hands became fists, and I longed to release their violence. When I'd calmed enough to think, I admitted that sins worse than fornication came to the confessional by the dozens. And I knew Mary hadn't sinned alone— she could not bear all the blame.

Yet I couldn't—wouldn't—offer the stupid girl absolution.

Davey was my half brother, and the family was poorer now than when I'd been Davey's age. I had cajoled and placated and pulled every string I could get my hands on to get Davey's name added to the regiment's rolls. Opportunity would not come twice to the boy's door, and the mortar Mary was prepared to launch on him could lay waste to his only chance.

Fury blew through me like a storm.

"Whore!" The word came up like vomit, and Mary's wordless cry only inflamed me more. When she tried to speak I spoke over her, my voice shaking, my eyes burning.

"Get out of my church Mary Evans. Get out! And wear your knees raw praying that God Almighty will end this evil of yours before the seed bears fruit."

It was near midnight Thursday night when Tamuel let himself into my office. He used the door, appeared in almost human form, and he spoke in a civil tone, all of which put me immediately on guard. The Demon adopted this approach when he meant to do business, and bargaining with Tamuel meant danger.

"I've a proposition, DuHarren."

"This is news?"

I grew more alarmed when he responded to my sarcasm with a lop-sided smile. Cutting straight to the gist, he said "You want out, old man, but you don't want to burn in Hell. Your chance has arrived."

I stared.

He rose, placed claw-fingered hands behind his back, and began to pace. Long years I'd been pacing just so. I saw now that it had been his habit I'd indulged, not mine. I pledged to pace no more.

"I'm tired of you," he repeated. He smiled as he paced, running his claws absently over the hearthstone. "Our red-haired friend, though—there's a man who interests me."

The priest had interested me, also. He'd reminded me—painfully—of the young man I'd been, long ago. Light where I was dark, compact where I was rangy, yet our souls were not so different. The Demon's interest couldn't bode well for him. Immediately when Tamuel spoke of it, I was beset with visions of young Father Michael caught for centuries in his claws and schemes.

Rather than examine the distress those visions caused, I forced a laugh. "Even if I agreed, Demon mine, do you suppose for a minute that Father Michael would consent to become my apprentice?"

"'Demon mine?' A fine attempt to bait me, but I won't bite." He sat again in the chair, crossed his arms, and commenced drumming his claws against his superfine wool jacket—my jacket, really. Gazing at me through narrowed eyes, he said, "I *want* that priest, DuHarren. And in answer to your question, I think his willingness is more possible than you believe. But that isn't what I have in mind. I've a simpler plan. We'll help him kill you, and then I'll teach him myself."

I choked on my indrawn breath, and the Demon poured me brandy and patted my back until I recovered. I thought at first I might cling to my existence solely to spite him. I could have done it. He was not allowed to kill me, and as I refused an apprentice, I could only be removed—and replaced— by murder.

Besides, though my life was burdensome, the remedy had drawbacks. Foremost, it condemned another soul to a loathsome existence, and the soul belonged to a man I'd rather not harm. Also critical, I'd be doomed to Satan's heat evermore—and that seemed a long time even at my age. Not least important, I found it daunting to contemplate my own murder.

Tamuel, demonstrating his skill at politic negotiation, had come prepared with a response to every objection. "And you've laid the groundwork," he concluded. "Your encounter with the priest unbalanced his mind."

He told me what Michael had said to Mary Evans. "After that, she went to the herb-wife for cure. She was convinced again that she must end the pregnancy but afraid to return here, thanks to your meddling. The herb-wife slipped, I'm afraid, and the poor girl died in a lovely pool of blood." Tamuel laughed, but he wouldn't confess to guiding the crone's bungling hand.

"Did you know," he asked me, "that Davey is Father Michael's youngest brother?" He smiled so broadly that it would have seemed joyous if it weren't for the countering effect of pointed teeth. "You laid the trap so cleverly, dear associate, that I won't believe you had no inkling of purpose."

He stepped close to embrace me, but I held up a hand and he stopped, prevented by our pact from touching my person without consent. My rebuff didn't dampen his jovial mood. "Three questions," he bellowed. "Three questions! I couldn't have planned it better myself."

After Mary's confession, my rage gave ground quickly to exhaustion. I gladly shed cassock and collar, fell on my cot, and slept that night long and hard. I woke Friday morning with the first grey gleam of day, hoping that what I seemed to remember about last night's confessional had been a dream. Out of habit, I bent my knees to the cold floor and began to mutter prayers, but I couldn't finish.

"Sweet Jesus, help me," I whispered, "I've condemned that girl."

I tended quickly to ablutions, vowing repeatedly never to allow weariness to cripple me again. I strode to the curb in front of the church, and was about to raise a still-clenched fist to hail a cab. My brother Davey stumbled from the alcove outside the chapel door and fell on my shoulder, wailing, dripping tears and snot.

"Michael, she's dead. My Mary's dead."

Dusk had fallen by the time I'd soothed Davey sufficiently, promising that I personally would bless Mary and see her buried in the churchyard. I hired a cab and accompanied him to the roadhouse, then left him to meet the postal coach that would deliver him to his regiment.

I directed the hansom's driver to DuHarren's establishment, and spent my time on the short trip staring out at the starless night and muttering about the sorcerer. "Abomination," I called him, and assured myself that Mary's blood was on his hands. That heathen had tricked me, had reduced me—a priest of God—to such a bedeviled state that I'd slaughtered a lamb in the confessional.

I checked my anger with a tight rein and laughed at what I saw as sublime irony. The sorcerer himself had given me the key to his undoing.

"Three questions," I said, my breath a mist in the cab's dark interior. "I couldn't have planned it better myself."

Friday evening I took from a drawer the silver dagger I habitually used to break a letter's seal, polished it bright, and placed it on my desk. That preparation done, I sat in my favorite armchair, feet stretched toward the hearth, and awaited Father Michael's knock.

Under the lamplight, I swirled a lovely amber liquid inside its crystal globe. It would be my last taste of peach brandy. Trying to get used to the idea, I ran through a list of final events as if reciting a litany. I would never again bathe in the sea, dash through the rain, join wills with a spirited horse, caress and claim a yielding thigh.

Pleasures I hadn't yet known were forever lost to me. The seasons would turn without my watch. And, I'd have not even another day to come to know my green-eyed priest.

This night, Tamuel and I would work hand-in-hand for the final few minutes of our long alliance, and at the end of it I would be free for the first time in two-hundred-fifty-three years, four months, and six days. A few breaths later, I'd also be dead, but I wouldn't feel the flames of Hell licking at my soles.

If the deed was done properly, the knife would suffice as a thumb in the breach. I'd breathe until it was moved or withdrawn. Between the act of murder and my demise, I'd have time to wheedle from the priest what I needed in order to escape Satan's donjons. Secretly, I intended to give Michael's soul an equal chance.

When I answered his knock, the young Father blazed through the foyer with holy zeal squealing at his heels, wagging its flea-bitten tail in anticipation.

"My third question," he demanded.

"Yes," I answered quietly. "It's that time. Will you take a seat? Some brandy?"

"Never mind your false civilities, DuHarren. I'm not here on social call."

I sighed. "Very well, then. Ask your question."

He gloated like the bird that nabbed the worm. "How can your sorcery be stopped?"

"Clever question," I said, though it was the most unsubtle question of all the millions that might have been asked on such an occasion. "Clever indeed, but the answer is simple. To stop me, you must kill me. Can you do it?"

To his credit, his face drained pale as a white peach upon hearing it, yet after a moment he nodded. Looking me square in the eye he said, "I can."

"There's more," I said. "The Demon Tamuel and I are bound by blood-sealed contract. He holds my heart in his grip, and you can't kill me unless the ties that bind it there are severed. My murder *must* be accomplished by piercing the left ventricle of my heart." I opened my shirt to show him the exact target.

"Just here," I said, "Do you understand?"

"Yes," he nodded. I saw no hesitation.

I thought I had banished fear, but suddenly every nerve and cell of my flesh rebelled, deaf to reasoning. Sweat beaded on my chest and dripped from my brow. Air seemed scarce—I couldn't find enough to fill my lungs, and when at last I did, I couldn't let it go. My hand shook wildly as I picked up the knife and placed the carved hilt in Michael's open hand.

The blade lay there for seconds, both of us staring at its gleam. Then, convulsively, Michael's fist closed around the hilt. I met his burning eyes and they told me what I knew. Our course was fixed. Nothing—nothing—could turn that dagger from my heart.

Nothing had ever fit my consecrated hand so perfectly as that silver dagger's hilt. I raised the blade between us. For an instant I held it there, suspended, while in my mind Mary's blood pooled and boiled at our feet, and then I thrust the blade toward DuHarren's lurid breast. Time lost all its markers, and I watched the subtle pulse of his flesh, each heartbeat a sweet eternity as the gleaming blade drew close. Then the tip pricked the skin and a single carmine droplet formed and fled the wound.

Alas for my humanity, I would have balked then, but Holy Spirit took hold and guided my hand. The knife, vehicle of God's vengeance, plunged into the heart of sin. So replete, so perfect was my communion at that righteous moment that my breath came hard and my blood pulsed hot and ecstasy seared my flesh.

Then, the heat drained from me all at once, running down my neck and back in rivulets. My cooled vision cleared—such a shock of icy change that I began to shiver. I felt DuHarren's eyes before I found them. The irises, once stone grey, had gone soft like soaked clay, and they drew me in. I passed through a *sorcerer's* eyes, but looked into a *man's* soul.

My hand shook and I heard him gasp, eyes wide in fear or pain. Still standing with me, he raised a hand and wrapped his strong, careful grip over my own, holding me steady.

"Easy, son," he said, pouring empathy I had never mustered even in ministry.

"A doctor . . ."

Tightening his grip, he said, "A doctor can't help."

"I've murdered you."

"You've freed me, Father Michael. I'm indebted to you. Yet I ask a final kindness."

I nodded through tears, my tongue locked.

Quickly, between sharp, short breaths, he told his story—a long, long life distilled into a few hard-edged sentences. At the end he said, "Please, Father, I don't want to burn."

Silent, I forced my thoughts into coherence. The wind began to howl outside and then a rumble of thunder and rain, hard rain. The candle on the desk bowed before a windy draft.

My voice came at last, thick with impossibility. "Were you baptized and confirmed?"

"Yes," DuHarren said, releasing his breath with a sound like leaves falling in November. "Yes, Christian is my given name." He made an odd sound, and I realized a beat later that it was laughter, full of humor but robbed of its heart, the knife in his chest chopping it into pained bits. "And my saint's name," he said, gathering control, "is Stephen, after the Martyr."

Scarcely thinking, trembling, I fumbled at the thong that tied my purse closed. "Help me," I said, and DuHarren's free hand partnered with mine. Together we draped my stole and readied the tiny flasks of oil and water.

"Confess."

He added his sins one upon the other like arithmetic and spoke the sum —a loose handful of words. I bade him pray with me and never had I heard even the most pious parishioner undertake a penance with such a joy of unburdening.

When the prayer was done, he repeated, "Amen." I cleared my throat to begin the rest, but he said, "Not yet, Father."

Hope thrilled over me, and breathless I asked, "Is there a way, then? Might you live?"

"No," he smiled. "Praise Heaven, no." Then his smile twitched and vanished, and for a moment his eyes burned once again. "You've saved me, Michael Carrick," he said, with as much force as the blade in his chest allowed. "Let me save you as well. Know this: The Demon Tamuel played guide to your hand tonight. He would bind you as he bound me."

The Demon, DuHarren said, had powers of persuasion that I couldn't imagine. I must gird myself with God and with whatever stonewalled defiance I owned. "He will ask three times before dawn," he told me. "You *must* refuse him every time."

He demanded my vow, his grip on my hand as strong as the iron that had once again hardened his eyes. When I gave my word, he sighed.

"Father," he asked, "Consecrated ground?"

"Yes."

"Pull out the blade."

We tugged together against the flesh of his heart, and suction gave way with a liquid rush. The blade came free. DuHarren crumpled, and I reached to soften his fall, letting the weapon clatter to the floor. His wounded heart embraced its own demise, shunting blood away in rhythmic spurts.

Last rites poured from my lips in time with that red pulse, sobs shaking my voice silent between floods. I finished the words as he died. He smiled at me until all the life had drained from his eyes.

I don't know where I found the strength in my small frame to carry DuHarren's body. The streets were darker than I'd ever seen them, all the lamps blown out by heinous wind, all the shutters latched against the storm, yet I made my way to the lich gate without stumbling. I laid DuHarren's corpse gently on unbroken sod, and left him alone while I went to fetch pick and shovel. I dug his grave deep, speaking comforts with every thrust and heave of the spade.

"Christian," I called him, "Christian Stephen, my son."

I first saw Tamuel as I left the cemetery, just as the bells of St. Martin's tolled midnight. He was formless, all darkness and shadow, but lit somehow from an inner core, a more beautiful monster than any I could have imagined. I asked him if this was his true form.

"Yes," he said, and his voice hissed like molten lead creeping over a glacial core. "Do you find it pleasing?"

"Evil," I said. "As is the beauty of Lucifer."

He laughed, and when he was through his voice had coalesced to a rich, rounded baritone. "Lucifer, eh? And what, pray tell, do you know of that old fraud?"

My labors at DuHarren's grave had purged me of heat, and I made no reply at all. It was only habit that rustled my fingertips over the beads of my rosary as he fell into step beside me, settled into near human form.

"No matter," he said, and stuck clawed hands into his pockets, hunching his shoulders as if cold. "But believe this: Lucifer's glory is like a candle in a house fire, compared to mine."

I noticed too late that he'd steered me away from the church and the priests' residence, where I had intended to take refuge until dawn and thus dodge the Demon's assaults. I noticed too that, though he was quite tall, our steps marked out time in matched rhythm, like old friends whose boots had kept company on many a long walk. I looked up to find the Demon's face, but—by all appearances—I walked the night streets with DuHarren.

He smiled.

"You're with me until dawn," he said a short time later. "No point in fighting."

A coach drawn by a pair of blacks waited at the apex of the River Bridge, and we boarded without ever a word to the driver. He took me to an inn on the edge of the city. In the dank hall, he ordered ale and bread and cheese, and set about making his pitch.

His first two offers proved easy to refuse. Promises of riches, power, and sex, descriptions of things he thought tempting—all of it made me conscious of the blood and grave dirt that soiled my clothes and my flesh. I wanted to add my vomit to the rest of the sticky substances on the rush-strewn floor.

He put aside his inkwell, quill, and parchment, and sat back to contemplate me. Pursing DuHarren's expressive lips, he drew down his brow as if puzzled and shook his head.

Dawn quivered just beyond the thinnest edge of night. I could hear it ringing like new-drawn steel. I thought that I had won.

"What would you change, Michael Carrick, if you could?"

"DuHarren," I said immediately, before I had a chance to raise my guard.

He laughed, a disturbingly gentle sound. "Alas! You pick the one deed even I cannot undo." A clock was ticking somewhere in the room, and the innkeeper's dog rose and stretched, ambled toward the door.

I waited for the cock's crow.

He asked, "What else?"

I wasn't going to answer. Yet dawn hung so near, what could it hurt? It would be a relief to confess my regret to someone, anyone, even the Demon Tamuel. Perhaps I pretended in that moment that it truly was DuHarren who sat across the rough-hewn planks of the table.

"Mary," I whispered. I cleared my throat and said it louder. "Mary Evans. I would undo that."

"Ah," he said. Still seeming kind, he produced bottle, quill, and parchment once more. He unrolled the scroll before me and I saw that the agreement was but a small paragraph. Below it stretched inch upon inch of parchment bearing one signature after another, each crossed out with a single neat line. As I watched, he dipped his quill in his well of blood-red ink, and scribed just such a line through the last name on the list.

Christian Stephen DuHarren.

I raised my gaze, expecting to look into the stone grey eyes that belonged to the man who had—in the end at least—owned that name. Instead, I saw green, my own too-liquid eyes—but dark as though through smoke over an olivine sea. I drew back, leaned away from that mirage as far as I could. The mirror eyes tethered my body there on the bench, but through my soul's eye I saw from a distance.

There I sat in the tavern light's glow, a hapless body housing a weak mind and a soul that craved the taste of every sweet evil I had renounced. But across the table breathed another me, a Michael Carrick with weakness smoothed from his brow, timid step made bold and sure, soft places girded with muscle. The things such a man, such a solid Michael Carrick, might do!

Light surged in those sea-gem eyes then, and drew me close until once more I sat body and soul across from Tamuel. As never before I loathed the cloak of my craven flesh, despised my heart with its cowardly tremble, endured my substance like torture. Tamuel reached his blunt-fingered, freckled hand—my own hand—across the age-polished oak, and I took it. My heart calmed, the tide of pain washed out. I did not receive strength, but I felt its promise.

Tamuel released me and showed me a likeness of my smile, then flattened the parchment open with one hand and elbow. With the other hand he dipped the quill anew and offered it to me, cocking an eyebrow.

"Well then," he asked, "for the good of our flock?"

~

Loretta Sylvestre lives in the rainy Northwest, where she harvests stories as they push up from the leaf mold in the dark of night. Her faithful cat, Badronymus, stands guard. She holds a BA from The Evergreen State College, but despite that she reads genre fiction and leaves books in her path like a trail of crumbs. She writes because she can't stop. Her stories have  *appeared in print and on the web in* SN Review, The Battered Suitcase, Tales from the Moonlit Path, *and* A Fly in Amber, *among other publications. She also works as an editor, and she blogs (sometimes) at* http://www.worldswellwritten.com.

Seeing Is

Craig Wolf

The sun was so hot it melted the telephone lines in strands of black licorice. Frying skillet sidewalks made ants scurry even faster than normal, dancing on their own pin-dot shadows. Cicadas buzzed like drowsy hornets trying to remember why they were angry. The sky was cloudless; the summer sun burned up anything that tried to sully the electric bright sky.

Jody strolled to the neighborhood pool, wearing only his neon blue swimming trunks, flip-flops, and a nylon net bag slung over his shoulder that contained his flippers, sunscreen, and towel. It was a nine-year-old kind of day, and he was fortunate to be just that age. There is no year like your ninth. Eight is okay, ten is fine, but neither is so right as nine.

He walked neither slowly nor quickly; his pace was that of his choosing. Time was as elastic as putty for Jody. Every day was as long as a year until it was almost over, when, like a rubber band, it snapped to a finish. So he walked as though his only purpose was to walk, and maybe it was.

He was halfway to the pool up at the community center when a voice, a harsh, whispering-a-dirty-secret-from-a-dark-alley-voice, *that* kind of voice, hissed out, "Hey kid."

Jody looked around. He did not jump. He was not nervous. If a pervert (which he thought might be his mother's current favorite word) was trying, in his mother's words, 'to pick him up,' big deal. Jody knew the guy'd have to be Vince Young to catch him. Faster than that. Faster than God maybe.

Unless he had a gun.

Yeah, as if.

He didn't see anybody, anybody at all, except fat old Mrs. Guidry almost a block away watering her grass by hand because she was too cheap to buy a sprinkler. Jody didn't think she had taken up ventriloquism as a hobby.

"No, kid, down here."

Jody looked down. There was a hole in the sidewalk the size of a milk cap, maybe a little bigger. Staring at him out of the hole was an eye.

An eye. *OK.*

Jody bent down to get a closer look.

Yeah, an eye. Iris the color of his mother's faded blue denim dress, pinprick pupil. Jody remembered "iris" and "pupil" from his life sciences class the year before.

How totally *crusty*.

"Who are you?" he asked it.

The eye rolled about as if seeking confirmation that no one else was nearby. "Never mind that, Jody."

Jody blinked. He knew he should not talk to strangers, but this was not a stranger, this was an eye.

"How do you know my name?"

"I know many things about you. Some of them are most interesting. Melissa Sherman, for example."

No one knew about his crush on Melissa Sherman. His friends would die if they knew he liked a girl. They would rag him forever. Longer.

"Hey, shut up," he told the eye.

The eye did not waver. "I know all about you, your mom, your dad, your uncle Brad and his meth bimbos and their cigarette burns—"

"Shut up!" Jody didn't like the . . . the eye talking that way about his Uncle Brad. Uncle Brad visited maybe three times a year and every time he did he brought Jody a new PS2 game. Better, Uncle Brad always played the games with Jody, and took him cool places, and wanted to go see the same movies Jody did and was just so all around cool, the coolest of his four uncles, and Jody wasn't gonna listen to some stupid eyeball slag him.

Now the voice of the eye became smoother, taking on a caramel slyness. "Did I touch a nerve there?"

Jody glared at it.

It rolled up and all Jody could see for a second was the white part, white with a crazy rootwork of red veins shot through it. Then it rolled back around and stared at Jody, only now the iris was brown. Dog turd brown, Jody thought.

"I do apologize," it said. "It was never my, ah, intention to . . . offend you."

Jody was not so young that sarcasm was unknown to him.

"Bite me," he said to the eye, and this cracked him up, really busted him out, because, well, it was just this eye, you know, and it couldn't *bite* anything.

"Listen to me, Jody, forewarned is forearmed. Seeing is believing. Knowledge is power. Leverage. Get used to it." It paused. "We could do much together, you and I. I know a great many things."

Jody stood up and turned away. Just a stupid ol' eyeball.

"Check in your father's desk drawer if you think I am making hollow boasts."

Jody froze.

"Go on. In the big tax code book he keeps in the drawer on the bottom right. In a beige envelope. Take a look. There's no need to see through a glass darkly, Jody."

Jody whirled about, but now the hole was just a hole, empty and dark.

Stupid ol' eyeball.

Jody went swimming.

Still, he could barely bring himself to look at his parents over dinner. He usually loved his mom's lasagna (veggie; she was on *that* kick again) but now he just picked at it. His dad seemed to know something was wrong and tried to get Jody pumped about the Rangers game they were driving over to Arlington to see Saturday, but Jody kept thinking about an envelope.

At last he excused himself, saying he didn't feel well, and he went to bed early.

He thought about his parents for a time. They were okay. His mom was prettier than a lot of other kids' moms, he knew that; even though she sometimes drove him and his dad up the wall with her fads, she was a good mom. His dad was a goob, not as cool as Nat Hofzinger's father, who was a cop, but nowhere near as bad as Forrest Blanchard's old man, who was the coach of their soccer team and whom Jody regarded as a total butthole.

His parents were okay. They really were.

So why couldn't he forget that envelope?

And there was his Uncle Brad. Meth bimbos? Cigarette burns? Jody could not get the ugly taste out of his mouth or his thoughts, and he knew that the next time his uncle came down to visit, it would be different. It just would.

Finally he accepted that he wasn't going to sleep until he knew. By this time night lights and shadows acted out alien plays on his ceiling. The house settled and popped. He could not get the envelope out of his mind. A dog barked off somewhere, and it nagged him. *Go see, go see,* it seemed to be saying.

When his clock read 3:13, he decided enough was enough.

His father's desk was forbidden ground. No one in the house ever said so, but it was all the same. Just like his Mother's top bureau drawer and Jody's footlocker in his room. Jody thought about it as he crept into his father's office and realized that everybody needed a private area, a secret place for private thoughts. Some kind of area that said NO TRESPASS.

He should stop, he knew that. Maybe that desk drawer was locked. If it was, then he would just go back to bed, say, "Oh, well, that's it, too bad." That's what he would do.

But of course it wasn't locked. Why should it have been? His dad trusted everyone to keep out.

Jody cringed as the drawer slid open. His heart flinched. But he had to know. He reached in and groped in the dark for the book. He found it immediately. It was a thick volume, full of arcane accountant stuff that Jody knew he'd never understand. He lifted it out and held it up by the spine, letting the pages dangle. An envelope, heavy with something inside, fell to the floor.

Jody put the book down and got the envelope. It was larger than the letter-sized ones he used for his pen pal in Scotland. He knew as soon as he picked it up that there were pictures inside. They were an old kind, thick with black backing on the back and some kind of deflated pouch at the bottom of that black backing. Jody didn't even know what kind of camera made pictures like these. Real old school stuff.

Moonlight poked through the blinds in the study, and Jody held the pictures up in the faint beams as he went through them.

It was his father, that was clear. Jody would know the face anywhere. But he looked so *young*. The girl (and that's what she was, maybe just old enough to drive) was unknown to Jody. He was old enough, had seen enough smuggled skin pictures on the school playground and crudely drawn graffiti down near the storm sewers where he and his friends sometimes played and even seen a series of pictures on his friend Nat's PC. He knew what they were doing. It had been some time since Jody had seen his father naked, and he had grown softer around the middle than he was in these pictures. There weren't a lot of pictures. In some of them, his father looked right at the camera, in defiance of shame. But in most of them he did not.

Jody put the pictures back as he had found them and stole back to bed, where he did not sleep a wink.

He did not walk by the hole in the sidewalk the next day, or the day after.

Three days after the sidewalk revelations, Jody got up early, having been plagued by terrible dreams in which he knew he was being watched constantly by God, who was a cruel Eye. He went to the kitchen to get a drink of milk and saw that the door to the garage was open a crack, the light on. He peered out and was just able to see his father holding a lighter up to the envelope and set the burning evidence down on the concrete. Jody watched the flames eat the pictures. As they became ashes, he glanced at his father, who could not look away from the smoke and flame. His face was torn by guilt and shame and self-loathing. He looked *old*. Jody backed away, stricken.

The next day, he rode his bicycle up to the Ace hardware store about a mile and a half from his house and with his allowance money bought a small, heavy bag of Quickcrete and placed it in his backpack. His dad had some of the stuff out in the garage, and Jody knew he could have used it, no prob, but it felt right to him that he pay his own.

When he got home with it, he found an old empty coffee can (his mother ground her own decaf beans now) in the garage and mixed up half a can of the stuff. He got a plastic cup out of the cupboard, one that had a lid. The one he chose was from a UT football game he and his dad had gone to last year. Hook 'em Horns. He placed this, the concrete patching mixture, and a rusty old putty knife that his dad would never miss into a plastic grocery sack, and went for a walk.

He stopped once, near a blocky power transformer, to agitate a nest of fire ants. He let dozens and dozens of them swarm into the plastic cup. They bit him twice, and it hurt, but he didn't react at all.

The eye was there, of course, and it started in on him the second it saw him. Today the iris was green, a tiger's eye.

"Jody! I am so glad to see you. Listen, your father, I wouldn't worry about that if I were you. It did him good. And he'll give you anything to keep you from telling your mother. You've got leverage now. Didn't I tell you? You should call your uncle. And you'll never guess what your principal does at night."

Jody set the bag down next to the hole. The eye flicked toward it, then back at Jody.

"What's that?" Not nearly so jovial now.

Jody said nothing. He removed the coffee can, the cup, the putty knife.

"What are you up to, Jody?"

The eye saw so much, why couldn't it see this coming? But Jody knew. It only saw the mean and nasty secrets. It only saw the worst. It only saw hurt. Well, what good was *that?* Sometimes looking through dark glass was best.

"Did you know that Ricky Traczyck still wets the bed? He does. Let him have that one next time he's pushing you around, see what happens."

Jody carefully took the lid off the cup, and quickly upended it over the hole, slamming the cup against the sidewalk. There was a beat, and then a muffled scream that, like the Energizer bunny, kept going and going. Jody tapped the bottom of the cup hard a couple of times. A stray fire ant crawled up the cup and bit his thumb before he could flick it away.

When the screaming subsided to sobbing, Jody lifted the cup away and tossed it behind him. There was little eye to be seen now, mostly just a seething mass of very ticked-off fire ants.

The eye screeched. "YOU LITTLE PUP! YOU UNGRATEFUL LITTLE WRETCH! YOU—"

Jody dug out a glob of Quickcrete from the coffee can with the putty knife and dropped it in the hole.

"HEY! HEY, YOU CAN'T—"

Another glob, and another, and then he couldn't hear it all anymore. He filled in the hole, smoothed the patch even with the sidewalk, and then, as an afterthought, found a twig and scratched his initials in the drying spot.

And then Jody went home.

~

This story originally appeared in the fifth issue of the late magazine Farthing *—allegedly. If any readers have actually* seen *this issue, the author would very much like to hear from you.*

Craig Wolf *lives and writes in the wilds of suburban Oklahoma City. He is the author of numerous short stories, as well as the collection* Pressure Points *and the novel* Trespass. *He is hard at work on a horror novel that might get him run out of his home state if anyone ever finds out what he's up to with it. More information than you could possibly want to know may be found at www.wolf-words.com.*

Afterword

. . . and that's our show, folks.

This is the sixth edition of the *Triangulation* anthology and the third that I've edited—third and final. I'm resigning from my post as editor.

I know that's the sort of statement that hints at all manner of behind-the-scenes drama, but in truth I'm stepping aside willingly. Both myself and Ann Cecil, the woman behind PARSEC Ink, agree that three years is probably enough for any one person to handle this particular gig.

Back in 2006 when I first took the job, I had a number of goals in mind. The first was that I wanted to move the anthology away from its regional orientation; the first three editions were limited to stories from writers somehow affiliated with PARSEC, the Pittsburgh-area science fiction organization. It's not that I felt there was anything wrong with the initial incarnations of *Triangulation*; far from it. My very first credit as a fiction writer came from the 2003 edition of the anthology, and I remain proud of it. I simply felt the idea had run its course; the 2006 edition failed to materialize in part due to a lack of material. I felt that if the anthology needed to grow if it was to survive.

In that, I feel I was successful. All three of the editions I've helmed have featured stories from writers all over the world. This year's edition alone drew close to five hundred submissions—true, small potatoes compared to the more significant short fiction markets out there (five hundred would be a slow month for, say, *Asimov's*), but enough for us to pick out some truly excellent stories. In terms of quality, I couldn't be more proud of the three books I've put together. (And if you'd like a copy of either of the first two for yourself, visit our website at ParsecInk.org, or go directly to the printer, Lulu.com.)

Second, I wanted to get the anthology more recognition, get some people who talk about fiction talking about *us*. There, too, I'm proud of what I've accomplished. As the both the front and back covers of this book attest, people are indeed talking about us. My underlying goal has always been to make this the kind of market contributors could brag about appearing in, and with favorable mentions in a variety of places, including *Black Gate*, *The Fix,* and *Asimov's*—freakin' *Asimov's*—I feel that's definitely something I can check off my list.

Third, I simply wanted the anthology to sell more. I had hoped that if I did a good enough job marketing this thing, my successor might not have to put so much of their own money into it.

Erm.

Yeah.

It turns out I'm a fairly lousy salesman. We've sold close to one hundred copies of each of the prior two editions, but I'm quite certain we can do better. I feel very strongly that the writers in these pages have written stories worth reading, and that I owe it to them to attract more readers. (And you who just got done reading those stories have my deepest thanks.)

Hopefully, Bill will do better.

Bill Moran will be taking the reins next year. Bill's been a member of my editorial staff for two years now, which I'm quite certain was more than enough time for him to learn both from my successes and my failures. The theme for next year's PARSEC short story contest will be "The Color of Silence." Will that be the theme of the anthology? That's up to Bill—as is every other detail, from writer payment to cover art to font selection. All I can say for certain is that Bill's a sharp guy and has been a tremendous help to me the past two years, and that I'm eager to read the anthology he puts together.

The *Triangulation* anthology has been an immensely valuable learning experience. Not only am I a better writer for the time I've spent as an editor, I have a much better understanding of what life is like on this side of the slushpile.

When you're puttering around the fringes of professional short fiction trying to get your own work sold, you hear a lot of stories about how writers are such incorrigible pains in the ass: thin-skinned, egotistical, prone to throwing temper tantrums should you dare speak ill of their work, that sort of thing. I wouldn't go so far as to say those stories are *false*—I had to hand out my first ban during this year's submissions—but I'll definitely say they're exaggerated. The writers I've worked with have been patient, reasonable, and thoroughly willing to discuss ways to make their work better. In short, the writers I've been fortunate enough to publish have, without fail, acted like *professionals*—even though the rate I pay stopped being "professional" sometime during the Eisenhower administration.

To all the writers I've published, and to all the writers who accepted rejection without pitching a fit (which is the overwhelming majority of you), you have my thanks.

And, as always, my thanks go out to Vinny Chong, for the kick-ass art gracing both this year's and last year's covers; to Ann Cecil, who gave me this wonderful opportunity in the first place; to my predecessors, Diane Turnshek and Barb Carlson, without whom this opportunity wouldn't have

152

existed; and to my editorial staff for helping me make the most of it.

To Joesph Benedetto, my best friend, a cagey old pro who's been at my side taming the slushpile since the beginning.

To Jamie Lackey, a formidably talented young writer whose wonderfully demented tale of Unicorns Gone Bad almost appeared in *End of Time;* my continuing friendship with her and her husband Paul Stefko remains the most valuable thing to ever come out of my slushpile.

To Bill Moran, my designated heir, a brother computer nerd and writer about to learn for himself both how much work this job entails and how much it will teach you in return.

And to Deanna Hardin, the Alpha Fangirl, whose exceptional taste and intelligence all but forced me to expand the size of my staff by one and who made me wish I'd had the sense to ask her to look over my shoulder from the first day.

I thank you all.

And now, if you'll excuse me, I have some lessons to apply to my own work. I've got a half-finished story about a dragon lying around here somewhere. . . .

Pete Butler
Penn Hills, PA, 2009

www.ingramcontent.com/pod-product-compliance
Lightning Source LLC
Chambersburg PA
CBHW051834170626
46807CB00003B/1172